FINDING ANGELO

The Wine Lover's Daughter, Book Two

ALSO BY CHRISTA POLKINHORN

NOVELS

The Italian Sister
The Wine Lover's Daughter, Book One

Fire in the Vineyard
The Wine Lover's Daughter, Book Three

An Uncommon Family
Family Portrait, Book One

Love of a Stonemason
Family Portrait, Book Two

Emilia
Family Portrait, Book Three

POETRY

Path of Fire

FINDING ANGELO

The Wine Lover's Daughter, Book Two

Christa Polkinhorn

Bookworm Press

Bookworm Press
1223 Wilshire Blvd., #1054
Santa Monica, CA 90403

Cover design: Diane Busch
Cover images: Andrushko Galyna, Bigstock.com

ISBN: 978-0-9600135-1-7

Printed in the United States of America

For my nephew Rico

PART ONE: A GRUESOME DISCOVERY

Chapter 1

Sofia narrowed her eyes as she spotted the two men. "They couldn't already be done," she murmured.

Her husband, Nicholas, and Martin, his grandfather, came walking across the meadow. They worked together with Matthew, Nicholas's younger brother, digging up their new field to prepare it for planting their Zinfandel grapevines. Perhaps they were just taking a break. Sofia went into the kitchen to prepare more coffee.

As she stepped outside to wait for the men, she discovered the first signs of spring—a patch of yellow daffodils in the corner of the patio that seemed to have emerged overnight. The shrubs of purple sage next to the now green meadows shimmered in the sun. A breeze came up, whispering through the grass and bringing a whiff of moist leaves. Stretched along the length of the hill above their home were their three vineyards.

After a rainy winter, they welcomed the sunshine of early March in San Luis Obispo County. The water was a godsend after years of drought, but the heavy rains during the last weeks had made it impossible to till the soil in their new field. Now, the conditions were perfect.

Nicholas and Sofia worked the three vineyards Nicholas's grandfather had owned in Paso Robles. The harvest of their Sangiovese, Nebbiolo, and Aglianico grapes last fall had been plentiful and the wine promised to be of excellent quality. Martin Segantino, a long-time successful vintner and winemaker, had more or less handed over his three grape varietals to them in exchange for a percentage of the profits from the wine sales. It had been a fruitful and mutually beneficial relationship.

Nicholas had always been Martin's favorite grandson. Both of them had similar ideas about winemaking. They liked to keep things simple, to work the vineyards the natural way with as little human interference and chemicals as possible. And this spring, the kind and generous man surprised them by gifting them the fields outright.

"It's time for me to sit back and watch you guys sweat while I drink a glass of your wine," he had said with a snicker and a twinkle in his eyes. However, he continued to help with the work and lent his experience and knowledge to them.

Nicholas's father, who owned the rest of the family estate, supported them as well. He had paid for the picking crew during the first few harvests.

The support from Nicholas's family, Nicholas's savings, and Sofia's contribution had made it possible for them to quit their other jobs and dedicate themselves fully to growing grapes and making wine.

The adventure had begun three years before when Sofia and Nicholas met on a vineyard in Tuscany. After Sofia's father died unexpectedly of a heart attack, she discovered a shocking secret. Sofia had known nothing about the double life her father had led for many years. He owned part of a vineyard in Tuscany and had a daughter there who was ten years younger than Sofia. Uncovering his hidden existence, meeting her sister Julietta and Julietta's Italian family for the first time had been a turbulent and emotional experience. Added to that, someone on the estate had tried to kill her to prevent her from inheriting her father's part of the vineyard.

Eventually, love and compassion won out and Sofia, Julietta, and the rest of the Italian family became very close. And best of all, Sofia met Nicholas, a young vintner from California, who worked on the estate in Tuscany. They fell in love and decided to pool their resources and work together on the vineyards of Nicholas's grandfather in the Central Coast area of California.

And here they were, enjoying the fruits of their labor. It was hard work, but Sofia enjoyed it. She had been an editor and writer for a wine, food, and travel magazine, and she still worked for them as a freelancer, writing occasional articles. But her focus was the vineyards she and her husband cultivated.

Sofia sipped her coffee while she watched the two men approach. They stopped halfway and from what she could make out, they were having an animated discussion. Nicholas waved his hands while his grandfather looked down at the ground, nodding occasionally. When they came closer, she saw immediately that something was wrong. Nicholas ran his hand through his blond hair. His honey-brown eyes looked troubled. His grandfather, a tall, skinny man in his seventies with short salt-and-pepper hair, was rubbing his lined forehead.

"What's the matter?" Sofia asked.

Their faces were somber. "There's a problem with the new field," Nicholas said.

"What is it?" Sofia put her cup of coffee on the garden table.

"We made a gruesome discovery," Martin said.

Chapter 2

"We found a bone … and it looks like a human bone." Nicholas reached for the coffee his wife had prepared for him and his grandfather.

"What?" Sofia stared at Nicholas and Martin. "How is this possible?"

"No idea. But it's really weird and it throws a wrench into our work. We called the police. I can't imagine what this is going to mean." Nicholas glanced at the hill above their house. The field in question was situated behind a group of oaks, a little farther away from their other three vineyards.

"God, I can't believe it. If the bone is human . . . a crime?" Sofia met Nicholas's eyes.

"Probably. I don't think that person buried him or herself voluntarily," Martin said. "I still hope it's an animal."

They looked at each other. "Perhaps someone is trying to scare us," Sofia said.

Nicholas grimaced, then smiled. "You seem to attract strange happenings. Did you bring danger with you from Tuscany?"

"That's not funny." Sofia gave him a playful punch. "What's going to happen now?"

Martin took off his baseball cap and brushed his hand over his short hair, then put the cap back on. "We'll just have to wait and see what the police say. Matthew called the cops. They're probably there by now. We better join them."

The three of them walked along the small path to the field, past a row of the ever-present oaks, which gave the town its name.

A couple of police cars were already parked next to the field. Officers were cordoning off the area with yellow crime tape.

"They're going to dig up the soil probably tomorrow to see if they can find more bones," Matthew, Nicholas's younger brother, told them.

One of the men was Walt Smith, the sheriff they all knew. He acknowledged their presence with a quick nod. "Whose field is it?" he asked.

"Ours." Nicholas pointed at himself and Sofia.

"How long have you had it?"

"Only for about three months." He turned to Martin who nodded. "Yes, the former owner is our neighbor, Frank Leonardi."

"Why would he bury bones?" Nicholas shook his head, trying to make sense out of this mystery.

"Someone else may have done it," Martin said. "I can't imagine Frank having anything to do with this. He certainly isn't a criminal."

Walt scratched his forehead. "Well, we don't know yet what kind of bone this is, although it does look human. The lab will tell more." He stared at Martin and Nicholas. "What makes you think this is a crime?"

Martin shrugged. "Fairly obvious, isn't it? I mean *you* are the police officer. Finding a bone in the ground that looks like a human bone doesn't exactly sound harmless, does it?" He motioned at the field. "After all, this isn't a cemetery."

"Not likely, no." Walt gave a half-smile. "Well, anyway, don't touch anything. Don't walk over the field. George Silver from the homicide division has been informed. He'll take over once the lab confirms the bone is human."

"How long is this going to take?" Nicholas asked. "We need to work the field, so it's ready in time for planting."

Walt looked him up and down. "Well, that's not the first priority now, is it?"

"For us it is," Nicholas snapped. "We already ordered the vines and once they arrive, they have to be planted right away or they'll be ruined. We do have to make a living, you know."

"I understand," Walt said in an appeasing tone. "If it turns out to be human, the whole field will have to be dug up to see if there are more bones or if this is a mass grave."

They all stared at him. "Sorry, bad joke," he said. "If the bone is from a human being, they'll have to find out who it belonged to. But this is out of my jurisdiction. I'm sorry, I can't be any more specific."

Nicholas took a deep breath. "Sorry, I don't mean to be rude. I know you have to do your job. It's just … well shocking."

"I understand," Walt said.

Nicholas was deep in thought as he, Martin, and Sofia slowly walked back to their house. "What a mess. I don't mean to sound callous. We don't even know whose bones they are. Perhaps there really was a crime. But I don't know what to do about the planting."

"I think we could still cancel the order of the vines," Sofia suggested. "Since we don't know how long this will take."

"Sofia may be right," Martin said.

"But we already organized everything, the workers, the back hoe … I don't mean to whine but …"

Nicholas felt his grandfather's hand on his shoulder. "I understand you're disappointed. So am I. But you already have three excellent grapes that will tide you over and keep you busy enough. So you have to wait another year to plant a fourth one. Think long-term, Nicholas."

Nicholas nodded. "You're right, Grandpa. I better not turn into my father." He was alluding to his father's "go-getter"-attitude. Robert Segantino was a vintner and winemaker in the grand style.

Martin shook his head. "Too much, too big, too complicated. It's not for me, but he seems to manage it. How? I don't know."

They lapsed into silence and walked quietly for a while.

"What worries me more than the field is the bone. I have a really bad feeling about what they're going to find," Martin said.

Nicholas glanced at him. "What do you mean, Grandpa?"

Martin hesitated, then cleared his throat. "Your great-uncle Angelo and Frank's brother, Fred, disappeared at the same time twenty years ago."

Nicholas stared at him. "You mean …?"

"I hope not."

"What's the story behind their disappearance?" Sofia asked. She put her arm around Nicholas.

"It's a long one. I'll tell you more later." Martin waved at them as he walked toward his home. Nicholas could tell his grandfather was worried. Normally he stood straight, but now his shoulders slumped a little.

"What is Grandpa referring to?" Sofia asked. She glanced at Nicholas, her purple-blue eyes concerned.

Nicholas put his arm around her slender waist and pulled her close. The sun caught the highlights in her light-brown hair. He brushed a strand out of her face and kissed her, then sighed.

"I don't know the whole story either. Grandpa has a younger brother by the name of Angelo. He was … well I guess still is the black sheep of the family. He was involved in some shady deals, and all of a sudden he disappeared. And Fred, Frank Leonardi's brother, was a close friend of Angelo's. He disappeared as well at about the same time. From what my father told me, they tried to find Angelo but had no luck. Grandpa doesn't even know if he's still alive."

"Did you know your uncle … I guess he would be your great-uncle?"

Nicholas wrinkled his forehead. "I barely remember him. He worked with Grandpa in the vineyard. I remember my father complaining about him being a no-good bastard and lazy. But he was always friendly to me. Anyway, nobody talks about this anymore … until now. I think Grandpa's worried that the bone in the field may have some connection to his brother's disappearance."

"Could it belong to Angelo?" Sofia asked.

"Oh, God, I hope not. Well, we'll find out eventually."

Chapter 3

"What are you thinking about?"

Martin felt a hand on his back. Maria, his wife of fifty-two years, smiled at him with her kind blue eyes. She had just come from the hairdresser. Her short, wavy, salt-and-pepper hair still smelled of hair spray, lavender he thought. He put his arm around her soft body. She was a little on the plump side but still beautiful. It was the kind of beauty that came from kindness and caring.

They had just finished lunch and were waiting for Sofia and Nicholas to come over for afternoon coffee. Martin gave a quick smile and continued to stare through the window.

The rain during the winter had revived the earth. The fields, which had been mostly yellow and brown during the past few years because of the drought, were now a lush green. It wouldn't last. Summer with its hot days would transform the colors into yellow, brown, rust, and purple. For now, green and the hues of the wild flowers dominated the landscape. But the beauty of nature didn't do much to cheer Martin up this sunny day in March. The news that the investigator, George Silver, had given him about the bones alleviated his fear that they belonged to his brother. However, it brought up new uncertainty and suspicions.

Martin sighed. "I'm glad the bones were not Angelo's. Thank God. But the fact that they belong to Fred really bothers me." He shook his head. "It must be awful for Frank to know that all this time, his brother had been buried on his property. His killer must be someone who had access to the field. I mean, it takes a while to bury a body."

Maria patted his back. "Angelo and Fred were involved in some illegal business. We know that. But this is a lot more serious. What about Fred and Frank's cousin? You know, the one who was in jail?"

"Anton, yes. Unsavory character. He was the one who gave Angelo a job. Fred and Angelo were drivers for his trucking company. No telling what they transported." Martin snorted briefly. "Still we don't know what really happened. And where is Angelo? Is he the killer? He has done a lot of stupid things but murdering someone?"

"Well, I don't believe it either. But here are the kids." Maria motioned at Sofia and Nicholas who came walking up the driveway.

Martin waved at them and opened the floor-to-ceiling glass door that led onto the patio and stepped outside.

Maria followed. "Want to sit outside? It's perfect today. I'll get the coffee."

"Let me help you," Sofia offered.

"Not necessary." Maria waved her off. "Just relax."

Martin sat down on one of the patio chairs while the others joined him. Maria brought a pot of coffee and a plate of cookies and put them on the table. She poured everybody a cup.

"So, the bones aren't Angelo's?" Nicholas said. "That must be a relief."

"Yes, this is the good news. But there's bad news, too." Martin dropped two cubes of sugar into his coffee and took a sip.

"Bad news?" Sofia asked. "What bad news?"

"The bones belong to Fred Leonardi," Martin said in his quiet, matter-of-fact voice.

"Oh, my God," Nicholas said. "Does Frank know?"

"Yes, he and I were down at the police station this morning. We met with George Silver, the investigator. He questioned us both."

"But you're not a suspect, Grandpa?" Nicholas asked with a grin.

Martin raised an eyebrow. "He called me a 'person of interest,' whatever that means. I'm supposed to stick around and be available for questioning. This is going to be a long investigation. They have to go back in time and try to reconstruct what happened back then."

"How do they know it was a crime? Couldn't it have been an accident?" Sofia asked.

"Hardly. Why would anybody bury a body in a field if it was an accident?" Martin glanced at Sofia.

Sofia gave an embarrassed smile. "You're right, of course."

"Besides," Maria said. "Didn't George say he was shot in the head?"

Martin nodded.

"How can they determine what happened after so many years?" Nicholas mused.

"Haven't you ever watched *Bones* on TV?" Maria said.

Nicholas shook his head.

"I've seen it a few times," Sofia said. "Quite interesting. I think they check the dental records."

"That may not even have been necessary." Martin took a sip of coffee. "They found an amulet Fred used to wear all the time and a ring. They also discovered a hole in the skull and that's how they know that Fred was shot. Well here is the person who knows more about this." He motioned with his head toward the driveway and got up.

A car parked and a man got out. "It's the investigator," Martin said. He waved. "Come through the yard. We're here." He watched as a man of medium height, robust figure, shaved head, probably in his forties, walked toward them.

The man's sharp gray eyes lingered briefly on each person. He nodded a greeting. "Hello. I'm Inspector George Silver."

Martin shook hands with him and introduced the family members to him.

"Want some coffee?" Martin asked.

Silver shook his head. "I'd appreciate a glass of water, though."

"I'll get it," Maria said.

Martin pointed at an empty garden chair.

"Thanks," George Silver said. "I just have a few more questions."

He gave a brief smile as Maria set a glass of water in front of him. "Thank you, ma'am." He took a sip of water, then turned to Martin. "From what Frank Leonardi told me, Fred and your brother Angelo were friends and often worked together. What can you tell me about their activities?"

Martin shook his head. "Not much I'm afraid. I know they were pals. They did some work together for a trucking company that belonged to Frank and Fred's cousin, Anton Leonardi." He watched Silver's reaction.

George Silver nodded. "Yes, Anton has had some dealings with the police. What about Angelo?"

"What about Angelo … that's a sad chapter." Martin ran his fingers through his hair. "My brother was … is ten years younger than me. He was a difficult child, and he got into all kinds of scrapes as an adult as well. I know he was involved in shady deals but if you believe he murdered Fred, no, I don't think so. They were good friends."

"Something may have changed in their relationship," Silver said. "Frank Leonardi feels that Angelo had something to do with Fred's disappearance."

"Then he knows more than I do. As far as I'm concerned, it was Fred who encouraged Angelo to work with him. Anton Leonardi, that's where you should focus your investigation." Martin felt the heat rise to his face.

"You can be sure, we're going to follow every lead," Silver said. "You told me you hadn't had any contact with your brother for twenty years? Did you never try to find him?"

"Of course I did," Martin snapped, then caught himself. "We all tried to find him. I filed a missing person report, but the police didn't do anything about it. See, Angelo left a note, telling us he was leaving and not to worry or try to find him. According to the cops, he was an adult who preferred not to stay in touch with the family and that was his right. They didn't consider this a missing person case."

"So what did you do?" Silver gave him an inquisitive look.

"What was I supposed to do? I went to New York where the letter was mailed from, hoping my relatives there knew something more. But they didn't. They admitted that Angelo stayed with them for a couple of weeks and then left. They suspected he may have gone to Italy, but they didn't know for sure."

"Why Italy?" Silver asked.

"Not sure why. The only reason would be that our family came from Italy. Our mother brought us here when we were kids."

"Are you still in touch with anybody in Italy?"

"No, I don't know anybody there. And Angelo was only three years old when we left. He wouldn't have any connections either. That's why I doubt he moved there. I don't think he even knows Italian." Martin shrugged.

"Anyway, after a while, I stopped looking. Angelo and I weren't on the best of terms anymore. I just didn't approve of his way of life. I was sick and tired helping him out and having him turn his back on us." Martin stared at Silver. "But I still don't believe Angelo had anything to do with Fred's death."

"Well, we need to find him." George Silver stood up. "Any information you can give us. If you hear anything from him or about him, let me know."

"Certainly. Believe me, now I'm as eager to find my brother as you are."

"Understand. Well, I'll be on my way. Thanks for the water." Silver got up and lifted his hand in a farewell gesture.

Martin rose and watched the inspector walk to his car and drive away. Just as he was about to sit down again, he sighed. "Oh, no, more trouble."

Chapter 4

"Frank's coming." Nicholas watched their neighbor walk up the hill.

"Yes, and he looks angry," Martin said, an anxious tone in his voice.

Frank Leonardi was a heavyset man, dressed in worn jeans, a wrinkled blue denim shirt, and work boots. He had curly gray hair. Nicholas figured he was in his sixties. His face was red and there were large sweat stains under his arms. Nicholas was afraid he would collapse and die of a heart attack.

When he got to the patio, he gave a brief nod to Maria, then faced Martin, flashes of anger in his eyes. "What did Silver want? What did you tell him?"

"Take it easy, Frank. Sit down. Want some coffee?"

"No," he snapped.

"What's the matter?"

"What's the matter?" Frank snorted. "I find out my brother has been buried in your field for ages and you ask me 'what's the matter?'"

"Wait a minute, Frank, that was your field until you sold it to Nicholas and Sofia three months ago. The bones were obviously buried there long before the field changed owners."

"Yeah, so? But where is your brother?"

"Frank, I wish I knew. I don't even know if he's still alive." Martin spoke quietly.

Frank's already red face got even darker. "I wouldn't be surprised if Angelo was the killer."

Martin narrowed his eyes. "Frank, this is a heavy accusation, and totally unjustified. Angelo and Fred were close friends. Why would Angelo kill him?"

"Angelo has been nothing but trouble, and he is at least in part responsible for the mess the two got in."

"Whoa, whoa, hold it, Frank." Martin's voice rose. "First of all, it was Fred who offered Angelo a job as a truck driver for Anton. I know that my brother was no saint but neither was Fred. And if you want to find a real criminal, then you should check out your cousin Anton."

"This is just like you, passing the buck. Anton has nothing to do with this. Besides, he doesn't even live here. He moved to Chicago years ago."

"But he was here when Angelo and Fred worked for him and then mysteriously disappeared," Martin said.

Frank glared at him. "All I know is that my brother is dead and your brother, who may have killed him, is alive somewhere. I'll tell you one thing. I'm not going to rest until this case is solved." He pulled a handkerchief out of his jeans pocket and wiped his face.

Martin got up. "Frank, I want this case solved as much as you do. I'm sorry about Fred, really. And I'll help in whatever way I can. But in the meantime, I kindly ask you to stop making blind accusations directed at me and my family. Let's please wait and have the police look into it."

Frank pushed his handkerchief back into his jeans pocket, turned on his heel, and walked across the lawn toward the street, muttering under his breath.

"That's too bad," Maria said. "I've never seen him this angry. He must be hurting because of what happened to his brother."

"Well, I don't know," Martin said. "I'm sure he's hurt, but he didn't seem to mind that Fred was gone. He didn't make much of an effort to find him. I just hope this isn't going to be a permanent break between us. After all, we're neighbors."

Nicholas had watched the argument between the two. He, too, was surprised at Frank's angry reaction. "You mentioned this Anton? What's his story?"

Martin waved his hand as if to swat a fly. "Anton Leonardi was in jail. Rumors have it that he's involved with the Mafia. I wouldn't put it past him. He's a crook. One of the bones of contention between me and Angelo was the fact that my brother started to work for him. I knew it wasn't legal work. Angelo had been doing better ever since he met Elvira, his wife, but all of a sudden things started going downhill again."

"Tell us about Angelo," Nicholas said. "I know so little about him … about you and your parents. I think I was nine years old when he disappeared. I remember him as a kind and fun person. He took me to the ice cream parlor a lot."

Martin nodded. "Yes, he could be loving and kind, but he had another, much darker side … but Maria, honey, didn't you say something about dessert?"

"Oh, God, yes. I forgot all about it because of Frank. I'll get it."

Sofia got up. "I'll help you."

"Thanks, Sofia, just get the plates. I'll bring the rest."

Nicholas watched as Sofia and Maria came back out with plates and a bowl of tiramisu. "Wow, Grandma, my favorite."

Maria dished out the dessert and poured each a fresh cup of coffee. For a few minutes, they ate quietly, then Martin pushed back his plate.

"My mother, your great-grandmother, came to the United States in 1950. I was thirteen and Angelo was three years old. My father was killed, supposedly by a mobster. I asked my mother about it, but she never gave me any details." Martin raised an eyebrow. "You know it's a stereotype to think that Italian immigrants have connections to the mob. I think the Godfather movie helped to cement our reputation. In the case of my family, however, it may at least have been partly true.

"We stayed with our relatives in New York. We were poor, but my mother worked hard, so that both my brother and I could have a good education. I did pretty well, but Angelo was trouble from the beginning.

"When our mother died—I was eighteen and Angelo was eight—things got worse. Losing his mother and father so early in life was really hard for him, well for both of us. I tried to take care of Angelo as best as I could. My cousins and my uncles tried to help, but they were all busy making a living. Angelo did poorly in school, didn't go to college, and, what was worse, began to hang out with the wrong kind of friends. He got arrested for shoplifting, fighting, the whole juvenile delinquent stuff." Martin took another sip of coffee.

Nicholas hung on every word he said. It was the first time he had gotten a more detailed picture of his grandfather's background.

"In college, I got interested in winemaking," Martin continued. "When I was old enough to be on my own, I moved to California together with Angelo. A friend of mine from college had started a vineyard near the Russian river."

"Really?" Sofia smiled. "My father and a friend of his did the same. In fact, we had a vineyard up along the Russian river. That was when my mother was still alive. Sorry for interrupting your story. Just reminded me. Go on."

Martin nodded. "Nicholas told me about your family's winemaking business up north."

"Anyway," he continued. "Eventually, we moved here. There was property for sale. This was at a time when the area was just beginning to become a well-known wine region.

There were only about three or four outfits. But for me, the climate and the soil were perfect. I wanted to grow some of the excellent Italian wines that weren't known very well in this country.

"At first, things seemed to work out. Angelo did fine for a while, but soon he kept slacking off and got tired of the heavy work. He wanted money and success without putting in the effort. Finally, I had enough and fired him. From then on, he kept doing odd jobs whenever something came up. Then he met Elvira."

"His wife," Nicholas said. "I do remember her. She was really nice."

"Yes," Martin acknowledged. "She was wonderful for Angelo. I've never seen him care that much about a person. And this inspired him to work harder. See, Elvira was a primary school teacher. She had steady work and made decent money. Angelo's pride was at stake. He didn't want her to be the only breadwinner. So he came back and asked me to take him on again. We were really busy at the vineyards, and I thought it would work this time. And it did … for a while."

"It was all thanks to Elvira." Maria ate the last bite of her dessert, then pushed her plate away. "But Angelo began to work odd jobs on the side again. We suspected it was illegal work, but we weren't sure. And then tragedy struck."

"Elvira? I remember she died," Nicholas said.

Martin cleared his throat. "Elvira was killed in a car accident."

"How terrible," Sofia said.

"Yes," Maria said. "Angelo was heartbroken. I've never seen him so desperate."

"Problem was, he felt guilty for her death. And in a way he was." Martin's voice sounded angry. "They had an argument, and from what Angelo mentioned later, it was about his jobs. They were fighting. Apparently, she took the car and drove off to visit a friend of hers at the coast. She must have been very upset and perhaps distracted. She lost control of the car and drove it over a cliff."

"Oh, no." Sofia exhaled.

"It was horrible. After that, Angelo seemed to disintegrate. He kept to himself and a couple of weeks later, he disappeared." Martin raised his hand and dropped it again on his knee. "I didn't even notice it at first. We tried to keep in touch but he completely withdrew."

"Didn't you say they lived in the house we live in now?" Nicholas asked.

"Yes, for a while," Maria said.

"The next thing I knew," Martin continued, "I received a note from New York from Angelo. It consisted of about three sentences and said he had to disappear for a while. He was okay and not to try to find him. I was angry at him … for everything. For spoiling his chance at happiness with Elvira by obviously getting involved in shady business again. For withdrawing completely and disappearing."

"We tried to find him," Maria continued. "We called our relatives in New York. They said he had stayed with them for a while, but then left. We don't really have much contact with the family in New York. One of Martin's cousins was a bad influence on Angelo. Well, I guess I may be somewhat unfair. Obviously, it didn't take much to get Angelo off the straight path."

"So you didn't hear anything further from Uncle Angelo?" Nicholas asked.

Martin shook his head. "No, nothing."

Nicholas caught Sofia's pensive look. He gently touched her face. She gave a quick wistful smile.

"This is just so sad," she said. "A brother lost for such a long time. It breaks up the family."

Maria and Martin observed her quietly. Nicholas felt she was thinking of her own sad family story, her mother's early death of a drug overdose, her father's secret double life.

Chapter 5

Sofia was sorting through a box of kitchenware and utensils Maria had left her. Since Sofia and Nicholas had lived in a small apartment for the last few years, they hadn't accumulated too many things and were now grateful for a few hand-me-downs from the grandparents.

A couple of months ago, they had moved into the charming old house that belonged to Martin and Maria. Several members of the Segantino family had lived in the house over the years. Sofia loved their new place, particularly the added space.

It was a rustic home with hardwood floors and wooden beams, a so-called half-timbered house, a style that was well known in northern areas of Europe, Germany and Switzerland, for instance. It had been built by an architect who was a relative of Maria's. Nicholas's grandmother was of German background and had always wanted a house in that style. As a child, she had spent many of her vacations with her German relatives on a farm in the Black Forest region and had fallen in love with the farmhouses there.

Sofia was admiring a colorful ceramic cake plate when a gust of wind rattled the window. It had rained off and on the past couple of days. The rain during the winter and early spring was only making a dent in the drought that had plagued California for several years. It wasn't enough to fill the diminishing reservoirs, but it was a good beginning.

The drought worried not just the government officials who tried to get control of the water shortage by means of a few controversial restrictions. Farmers, winemakers, and the tourist industry all agreed that something had to be done but had different opinions as to how the problem was going to be solved. There had been some acrimonious exchanges between the different factions of the otherwise peaceful communities in the drought-stricken Central Coast of California. Some people blamed the proliferation of vineyards in the area for the water shortage. Members of the wine industry, however, felt the blame was one-sided and unfair. According to the vintners, vines and grapes needed little water during the growing season, much less than for instance alfalfa and almonds, and they needed almost nothing when the grapes were ripening. Sofia agreed with the vintners but also felt that the increasing number of huge vineyards added to the problem.

Sofia carried a box downstairs, unpacked the dishes and towels, and put them away. She and Nicholas wanted to convert the den upstairs into an office. Adjacent to it was a storage room with a few pieces of old furniture that belonged to Martin and Maria as well as a collection of boxes of items left by several members of the family who had lived in the house over the years. Sofia wanted to pull out the lighter boxes and put them downstairs, so the owners could pick them up or discard them. A few of the boxes were labeled and some were unmarked. She went upstairs again and opened one without a label to find out who it belonged to.

On top in the box was a framed photograph of a man, perhaps in his thirties or early forties. Sofia thought first that it was Martin. At closer examination, however, she saw that it wasn't him. The man in the picture had piercing dark eyes while Martin's eyes were a soft honey-brown just like Nicholas's. Sofia gave a quick gasp and her heartbeat increased as she realized that it must be Angelo, the lost brother, and that the box belonged to him or to his wife Elvira.

Sofia stared at the photo for a while. "Where are you, Uncle Angelo?" she whispered. "What have you done? Are you still alive? Are you guilty? Or just afraid?" Sofia knew from experience how a dark secret can hurt and even ruin a family.

She put the photo aside and began to browse through the rest of the stuff. There wasn't much, a pile of envelopes held together with a rubber band, a blouse, jacket, and a skirt, things that belonged to a woman. At the very bottom, hidden under a blanket, was a notebook or diary. It reminded Sofia of the diary she'd had as a child, but this looked more as if it belonged to an adult. It was of dark-blue leather and had a golden lock. Sofia checked to see if there was a key somewhere but couldn't find one.

Outside, the wind picked up again. A slamming door downstairs startled Sofia. Then she heard Nicholas's voice.

"Darn it. It sure blows, knocked the door right out of my hand. Where are you?"

"Up here," Sofia called back. "Come and look."

After a moment, she heard his footsteps on the stairs. Nicholas was back from working at the winery together with his grandfather.

He kissed her on the head and knelt down next to her. "What's this?" He pointed at the box.

"I'm cleaning out the storage room and I found a box that seems to belong to Elvira or Angelo. Most likely Elvira, since these are women's clothes." She picked up the notebook and handed it to Nicholas. "This was in it."

He took it from her and turned it around. "Is there a key?"

"No, I didn't find one," Sofia said.

"I'm sure it's easy to break open." Nicholas began to fiddle with the lock.

"Shouldn't we ask Grandpa and Grandma first? It doesn't belong to us."

Nicholas stood up. "If it belongs to Elvira, it may be important. It may say something about Angelo. Of course, we'll give it to Grandpa. But let me see if I have something to open it without breaking the lock."

Nicholas went downstairs and came back up with a tiny screwdriver with a thin blade. He stuck it into the keyhole of the diary, jiggling it a little. After a few attempts, the lock sprung open. "Not much of a security device," he murmured.

He opened the book and began to page through it with Sofia peering over his shoulder. They read the first entry, then glanced at each other, stunned.

"It does belong to Elvira," Nicholas said. "And here she writes something about Angelo." He handed the diary to Sofia.

"My God," Nicholas said. "This may tell us something about what happened back then. You're right, we better tell Grandpa and Grandma. What else was in the box?"

Sofia looked up. "A photo, I think it's of Angelo. And a bunch of envelopes. Must be letters."

Nicholas examined the photo. "Yes, this is Great-Uncle Angelo. Wow. That's how I remember him. He had these black eyes that seemed to burn you when he was angry. Fortunately, he wasn't angry a lot, at least not at me. I liked him." Nicholas smiled. "I hope he's still alive and okay. I'd love to see him again."

Sofia pulled out the bundle of envelopes. The rubber band broke when she tried to pull it off. It was obviously old. She opened one of the envelopes. There was a piece of paper in it, a letter. Sofia began to read, then stopped. "These must be letters from Angelo to Elvira. Look at the signature and the date."

"Oh, my … this was in 1988, you're right, this is from Angelo. Let's take this to Grandpa and Grandma." Nicholas looked at his watch. "They're probably having lunch."

"Definitely my brother." Martin stared at the photo. "This must have been before they got married. He still had longish hair. He cut it short later." He handed the photo to Maria and picked up the diary, paging through it. Maria looked over his shoulder. Nicholas and Sofia stood next to her. Sofia leaned over, trying to catch a glimpse.

"Boy, this is amazing. Thanks for finding this." Martin glanced at Sofia. "This may be a treasure … not in the usual sense, but it may help us find out what happened to Angelo.

"I'll read the diary and then you can have it as well. We also have to give it to George Silver." Martin opened the book again and began to read quietly.

Sofia hoped he was a fast reader. She was really curious about the diary.

"Well here is something." Martin raised his head. "As I suspected, my no-good brother was involved with a bunch of criminals."

Chapter 6

Maria sighed. She had hoped her husband would find something positive in the diary, but that had been wishful thinking. She felt sorry for him, knowing that he was torn between love for his brother, sadness at having lost him, and disappointment in him and the way he had conducted himself.

Martin slapped the diary on the table. He looked upset. "This is going to be difficult reading." He paged through the book. "Fortunately, it's not too long. I should be able to finish it today or tomorrow, and then you can have it." He picked up the book again and kept on reading for a little while. Then, to everybody's surprise, he handed it to Maria and Sofia.

"Go ahead. You two read it first. I don't have the stomach for it today." He got up and walked to the window.

"Well, Sofia and I were going to do a little work at the winery," Nicholas said.

"Come on, I'll help you." Martin put a hand on Nicholas's shoulder. "I can't sit still right now. Let the ladies do the reading."

"Okay, Grandpa, if you don't mind," Nicholas said. "I just want to take a tour through the vineyards to make sure everything is okay."

"Thanks, guys," Sofia said. "I really want to read this, and I'm sure Grandma is curious, too."

Maria nodded. "Yes, let's read it together. We'll take turns and read it out loud."

Nicholas and Martin left and the two women poured themselves another cup of coffee.

"Why don't you start," Sofia said and handed Maria the book. Maria began to read silently. "This is just everyday stuff, nothing alarming," she said. After a few pages, she looked up. "Here is something." She read out loud.

Yesterday, Angelo and Fred were out all night again. Working for Fred's cousin, Angelo said. They have been gone a lot lately. Angelo never gives me any details about this so-called work. He just says that they work for Anton's trucking company, delivering goods. Why at night? And why can't he tell me what kind of goods? When I ask questions, Angelo says to stop worrying, that the money is good and we can certainly use it. I told him we have enough money with what he makes on his jobs and my salary and benefits. Whenever I mention my work, he gets angry. He tells me he doesn't want to live off my money. What an outdated attitude. He is such a male chauvinist sometimes. What's wrong with the woman making more money? It makes me mad. And I'm really worried.

I'm worried that he's involved in something bad. I know about his past, about his juvenile record in New York. I'm afraid he's picked up those bad habits again.

"Stupid male pride," Maria said, irritated. "He wanted to be the bread-winner, but he didn't want to do the heavy work of a legal job. Martin and even Robert and his family gave him so many chances. But no, he wanted the fast money, no matter where it came from. Disgusting." She put the book down and glanced at the meadow in front of their house.

"It must have been so hard for Elvira," Maria continued. "She was a wonderful person and she really loved Angelo. That's what made us so angry at him. After messing up so badly, he met this woman and he had the most wonderful luck. And then he went ahead and ruined it again. And her in the process." She picked up the diary again and gave it to Sofia.

Sofia smoothed the page, and began to read.

I confronted him again about his being out at night. I asked him if he was having an affair. He seemed genuinely shocked. He told me no, that I should know he loved only me. "Then why all the secrecy?" I asked him. He said he couldn't talk about it, that it would put me in danger, but he assured me it had nothing to do with another woman.

At this point, the entries stopped for a while. The next entry was a few weeks later. It was more disturbing news.

Angelo told me that during one of the jobs delivering goods, they witnessed a crime. A man was shot. The killer saw them. Angelo didn't tell me who the killer was.

I was terrified. I asked Angelo why they didn't go to the police. He said they couldn't. They wouldn't believe him. The killer was a powerful man. And the work Angelo and Fred did was illegal. They didn't know it at first but found out later. So if they went to the police they would end up in jail as well.

Maria lifted an eyebrow. "They didn't know it was illegal? A likely story. Of course they knew." She took over the reading again.

Then who was it? I asked him. Was it Anton? He said he had already told me too much. He warned me not to tell anybody about this. If I did, I and the whole family could be in danger. He also told me that he might have to disappear for a while and to not worry about him.

But I'm so worried. I wish I could tell somebody.

That was the last entry in the diary. Sofia and Maria looked at each other stunned.

"Too bad, Elvira didn't find out who the killer was," Maria said.

Sofia closed the diary. "We definitely have to give this to the investigator."

"Give what to the investigator?"

Maria flinched at the booming, angry voice. She and Sofia turned. Frank Leonardi stood in the doorway.

"I knocked and nobody answered. I heard voices. The door was open." He entered and stood next to Maria, his heavyset body looming over her.

Maria glared at Frank. "You still could've tried a little harder to get our attention. You don't just barge into somebody's house."

"Yeah, especially when the people inside do something illegal."

Maria's anger flared at Frank's rude behavior and his accusations. "We haven't done anything illegal.

"What's that?" He pointed at the diary.

"This is something we're going to give to George Silver," Maria said.

"I want to see it. Give it to me." Frank's voice sounded threatening.

"You'll get it in time." Martin stood in the doorway next to Nicholas. "Now please leave and never talk to my wife and great-niece like that again."

"This isn't over with." Frank shoved past them and stormed outside.

"You're damn right, this isn't over with," Martin called after him in an unusually loud voice. He let himself fall into a chair. "I've had it with that guy."

Chapter 7

"How would you like to go on a short vacation to New York City?" Nicholas murmured. Sofia glanced at his face in the diffuse sunlight that shone through the blinds in the early morning. "You know, we never had a real honeymoon. Too busy working," he continued.

"New York for a honeymoon? Doesn't sound very romantic. Why New York?" Sofia moved closer to Nicholas's side of the bed.

"Well, okay, I have an ulterior motive as well." Nicholas kissed her. "I thought we could also visit the Segantino family in New York. The last time I saw them was … well a long time ago. I was there once with my parents as a child."

"Ah, now I get it. You want to snoop around and ask them about Angelo." Sofia touched his smooth chest. "Good idea, actually. Grandpa hasn't been the same since we found the bones. He's worried. He must miss his younger brother. I mean even if he wasn't a model citizen, he's still his brother."

"I know. That's why I thought we could do a little investigating. Besides, I really want to go back to the city once again. I mean it is an interesting place. All the museums, art galleries, skyscrapers, the Village, Rockefeller Center. It would be fun."

"Why don't we coordinate the visit with my trip to Italy?" Sofia suggested. "I can book the flight so I have a stopover in New York."

"Oh, yeah, that should work. I'm going to miss you when you go to Italy." Nicholas sighed. "I wish I could come with you, but work, you know."

"Yes, I know. I won't be gone for too long. But I'll miss you, too." Sofia snuggled up to him. "I'm so looking forward to having Julietta with us in the fall."

"I agree, that will be great. I hope she'll like it at Cal Poly," Nicholas said.

"I'm sure she will. She was all excited when she saw the pictures of the campus. It will be very different from the more or less purely functional university in Italy she's attending right now." Sofia stretched and yawned. "We probably should get up."

"Not yet, weren't you saying something about a romantic honeymoon. I mean we can create romance right here." Nicholas put his hand on her breast and gently squeezed her nipple. A zing of desire shot through Sofia's body. She wrapped her arms around him.

"Oh, no, it's getting late," Sofia said as she woke from dozing off again. The sun had fully risen and was bathing the bedroom in a golden light. Sofia stretched and yawned, got up, and gave the still sleeping Nicholas a playful slap on the behind. "Come on, sleepyhead. I bet you Grandpa is already at the winery."

Nicholas groaned, then pushed himself up with his arms and gazed at the window. "Darn it, you're right. He must think we're a bunch of lazy bums." He brushed through his tousled blond hair. "Well, I guess since the vineyards belong to us now, we can decide how early we start with the work." He grinned. "But around Grandpa I still feel like the apprentice who has to prove himself. Although I really have no reason; he never put a lot of pressure on me … not like my father."

"Was your father strict?"

"Not really, but he was a doer. He was … well, still is … all action. Grandpa is more relaxed, but he's also a hard worker. He just doesn't push you all the time."

In the kitchen, Sofia filled the espresso pot with water, pushed the button on the coffee grinder, and inhaled the smell of freshly ground coffee. After a while, the kitchen filled with the aroma of dark espresso.

After a quick shower and a cup of coffee, Sofia poured the rest into a thermos and grabbed a couple of granola bars for breakfast. They walked the short path down the hill past the vineyards to the winery.

"Sure enough, there he is." Sofia waved at Martin who was making his way slowly through one of the rows of the vineyard with the Sangiovese grapes, checking the vines.

Since there was no grass planted along the rows of the vineyards, walking on the soft dirt and sand was somewhat of a challenge, but it helped to conserve the precious water. Martin had decided not to plant grass long before the drought became a problem. He had always felt that it was an unnecessary waste since grass and lawns needed to be watered regularly.

After a while, Martin joined Sofia and Nicholas at the winery. Sofia and Nicholas were in the process of racking the wine from the Nebbiolo grapes. They had attached the hoses from the barrels with the aging wine to the fermentation tank. The juice without the sediments was siphoned into the tank and stayed there overnight. In the meantime, the empty barrels needed to be cleaned and sanitized thoroughly so no unwanted yeast or bacteria collected, which could spoil the wine.

Three of the now empty barrels were sitting on a contraption with a large container to catch the water underneath. Nicholas and Sofia were each cleaning one of the barrels with a high-pressure cleaning device. Martin took hold of a third one and proceeded to clean it.

"Thanks, Grandpa," Nicholas said. "We kind of overslept."

Martin smiled but didn't say anything, and Sofia felt herself blush.

"New York?" Martin asked after Nicholas told him of their plans. "What do you want in New York?"

"Sightseeing, mainly," Nicholas said. "A short vacation before Sofia goes to Italy. Besides, we could visit our relatives once again. I was only there once with my parents, and I remember they seemed to be a bunch of funny, slightly nutty people."

Sofia watched the old man's serious expression.

"This wouldn't happen to have anything to do with finding out about Angelo?" Martin asked.

"Well, it wouldn't hurt to ask if they have any news," Nicholas said.

Martin shook his head. "I don't think they do. I called them right after we found the bones and asked them."

"Oh, really?" Nicholas said. "So you thought that the bones might have something to do with Angelo?"

Martin sighed. "I just had a bad feeling about it. As it turns out, I was right. Not about the bones possibly belonging to my brother, which I feared at first. But he is somehow involved, as we found out from Elvira's diary.

"Anyway, if you're going to New York because you think you can find out something about Angelo, you'd probably be wasting your time. When I tried to find Angelo years ago, my relatives weren't of any help. Either they didn't know anything, or they had no intention of telling me. They knew Angelo and I didn't get along." Martin paused. "Problem is, at least one of my cousins was less than clean when it came to the law. I blamed him in part for leading Angelo astray."

"Which of the cousins is that?" Nicholas asked.

"Giuseppe," Martin said. "You probably don't know him."

"I think I met him. Isn't he the fat one—at least he was fat then—with the dark curly hair and the mustache. He had this heavy Italian accent and he was always joking around. He was funny."

"Yes, that's probably him. He can be funny all right, but I wouldn't trust the guy if my life depended on it," Martin said.

Sofia grinned. "Little did I know when I met Nicholas that I was marrying into a family of criminals." She patted Martin's arm, hoping she hadn't offended him. "Just kidding, Grandpa."

Martin gave a quick smile. "Yes, you should have made some inquiries first. We Segantinos sure have a few skeletons in the closet. Well, at least in the vineyards."

Then he turned serious again. "I hate for you to get into trouble, snooping around. I don't trust my relatives. This isn't your business, Nicholas. Let's leave it to the police."

"Don't worry, Grandpa. We're not going to do anything dangerous. And this really isn't the main reason for our trip to New York. It would just be nice to spend a few days with Sofia doing something fun, before she goes to Italy … and before the heavy work at the vineyards starts again."

Martin nodded. "That's fine. I can take care of things here for a few days."

"Thanks, Grandpa." Nicholas said.

Martin turned to Sofia. "Perhaps one of these days, Maria and I can take a trip to Italy. I wouldn't mind seeing your vineyard in Tuscany. Sounds like a wonderful place."

"That would be great," Sofia said. "My family there would really enjoy having you."

PART TWO: A FAMILY IN TROUBLE

Chapter 8

JFK Airport in New York was a mess. A winter storm created chaos. Flights were canceled or delayed. The plane from San Luis Obispo Nicholas and Sofia were on was delayed but, fortunately, able to land. Now, they were in the arrival hall, waiting for one of their relatives who was supposed to pick them up. They had been waiting for half an hour.

"Not knowing what the guy looks like doesn't make it any easier," Nicholas mumbled as he scanned the people walking in and out of the arrival hall. "He said he'd hold up a sign."

"Perhaps he was delayed because of the weather," Sofia suggested.

"But it isn't snowing here," Nicholas remarked.

"No, but it's windy." Sofia motioned at the fluttering flags on top of one of the airport buildings. "I'm getting hungry." She pointed at a snack bar. "Perhaps they have a sandwich or something. We can watch the people from there."

Nicholas nodded. "Okay, and if he doesn't show up by the time we're finished, we'll just take a shuttle or a cab and go to our hotel. We can call them from there."

They ordered juice and sandwiches, then sat down at a table from where they could keep an eye on the people coming and going.

"Well, Martin must be right about his New York relatives," Nicholas said after he finished his snack. "They don't seem to be very dependable. Why don't we just leave? I'm tired of waiting."

Sofia agreed. They grabbed their luggage and headed for the exit. Outside, they boarded a shuttle to the Port Authority station at Times Square in Manhattan, and from there they took a cab to their hotel near the Guggenheim Museum. After checking in and depositing their suitcase and bags in their small but clean room, Nicholas tried again to call the Segantino family on Staten Island. After a few rings, a woman answered. Nicholas told her who he was.

"What? You're here already? Oh, my God. Wait a minute … Mario," she shouted.

Nicholas began to lose heart. He rolled his eyes and looked at Sofia. At this moment, someone at the other end coughed.

"Hi, this is Mario. Nicholas?" a male voice said.

"Yes, it's me. I'm sorry, we waited for quite a long time at the airport, but nobody came."

"Oh, no." Mario sounded upset. "I thought it was tomorrow. Sorry about that. Where are you now?"

Nicholas gave him the name of the hotel in Manhattan.

"Sorry again. Why don't you come here tomorrow? I can pick you up."

"Well, Sofia and I can take the ferry to Staten Island," Nicholas said. "We've never done this before. Sounds like a fun trip."

"All right. Check the schedule and give me the time when you arrive in Staten Island. I'll pick you up. Call my cell." Mario gave Nicholas his mobile phone number.

"Okay, see you tomorrow. Don't forget," Nicholas said.

"No, man, I won't. Promise. See ya." Nicholas heard a titter, then pressed the disconnect button. "Well, at least one person in that family seems halfway dependable."

Sofia laughed and patted his shoulder. "You're starting to sound like your grandfather."

"So, what are we going to do with the rest of the day? Museum?" Nicholas put on his jacket.

Sofia grabbed her purse. "Yes, let's go to the Guggenheim."

It was only a few blocks from the hotel to the museum. When they arrived, they admired the architecture of the modern building right next to Central Park, designed by Frank Lloyd Wright. They checked out the exhibitions and decided to just go into the general one.

"Whoa, pricey," Nicholas said, as he saw the entrance fee. "A lot more than the museums in Los Angeles and San Francisco."

"Well, we're on vacation and this is a very special museum," Sofia said.

They walked on the slowly rising path along the rotunda, admiring the works of art and enjoying the special atmosphere the organic form of this building created.

"It *is* amazing," Nicholas whispered, squeezing Sofia's hand.

In the evening, they went to have dinner in a restaurant near their hotel.

"I really wonder what these relatives of mine are like," Nicholas said. "I don't remember them very well. I was a boy when we visited them in New York."

"I'm curious, too," Sofia said. "Grandpa doesn't seem to think very highly of them."

"That's true. Well, we'll see." Nicholas took a sip of wine. He grimaced slightly. "The food is good here, but the wine … a little on the bland side for a Merlot."

"You can't expect all the wines to be as excellent as ours." Sofia snickered. "Don't I sound like one of these wine snobs?"

After dinner, they went for a walk, then returned to their hotel. Nicholas tried to call Mario again to give him their arrival time at Staten Island the following day. Instead of Mario, a woman answered and told him that Mario couldn't come to the phone right then. "Can I leave him a message?" she asked.

Nicholas gave her the arrival time of the ferry. "Make sure he gets the information," he added.

"Yeah, sure, no problem." The phone disconnected, before Nicholas could say anything more.

"Hmm. Not very reassuring," Nicholas said. "We can only hope Mario gets the information."

"Don't worry. Whatever happens, at least, we'll have a nice outing on the boat," Sofia said.

"I guess I should call Grandpa. But I better wait until tomorrow. Perhaps we'll have something more definite to tell him," Nicholas said.

"Time to go to bed?" Sofia put her arms around him.

"Sounds good to me. As long as it's not just for sleeping." Nicholas kissed her and she gave a pleasurable sigh as his hand moved over her body.

Chapter 9

After a quick breakfast, Sofia and Nicholas took the subway to the Whitehall Terminal in Lower Manhattan. They got the tickets and waited for the boat to Staten Island to arrive.

"This is great," Sofia said as the boat was leaving the harbor. "Now, we'll have a view of New York from the water." It was a pleasant surprise for her. Here was Manhattan in its glory, including the new tower on Ground Zero where the terrorists had destroyed the twin towers of the World Trade Center. Sofia felt the new structure was a little over the top—interesting but too grandiose. Nicholas agreed. However, they enjoyed the view of the Statue of Liberty, the Hudson River, and the surrounding area.

Sofia gazed eagerly toward Staten Island, which became visible as the fog lifted. "It's nippy," she said, zipping up her down vest and hugging her arms.

"Let's go inside," Nicholas suggested. They went into the cabin and sat down next to a window.

The ride took about thirty minutes. When they arrived at the station on Staten Island, they got off the boat and waited in the entrance hall. Mario had told Nicholas he was going to hold up a sign with the family name.

"There he is." Sofia motioned with her head toward a young man holding up a cardboard sign with *Segantino* written on it.

Nicholas waved and the man started toward them. He was about Sofia's height, slim, with longish dark hair that curled slightly over the collar. The color of his hair and his dark brown, almost black, eyes reminded Sofia of the photo she had seen of Angelo. He was definitely part of the Segantinos. She judged him to be in his thirties.

"Hi there. I'm Mario." He hugged Nicholas and slapped him on the back. He looked Sofia up and down and smiled. "Pleased to meet you. So, you are the beautiful wife." He hugged her, then stepped back.

"Sorry, guys, about missing you yesterday. I don't want to pass the buck, but Uncle Giuseppe gave me the wrong date."

"No problem," Nicholas said and gave Sofia a quick glance.

They left the terminal and Mario pointed his key at a sporty-looking BMW to turn off the alarm. *He must be wealthy,* Sofia thought.

"Sorry about the mess." Mario grabbed a bunch of books and a few empty Starbucks coffee paper cups. He threw the cups in a trash bin nearby and tossed the books onto the back seat. "Just move them over," he said to Nicholas who opened the back door.

"Are you an engineer?" Nicholas asked as he picked up one of the books. Sofia, sitting in front, turned to glance at the title, something about electrical engineering.

"Yeah," Mario said. "I'm one of the few members of the family who went to college. I work for a company called Arup. It's a good place. Lots of opportunities for continuing education." He started the car and drove along a narrow road, then eased his way onto a freeway going south toward Rosebank where the family lived.

"So, how's life in California?" Mario asked.

"Busy but great," Nicholas said.

"I really want to visit you guys sometime. I was in San Francisco on business last year, but I was too busy with work." Mario shrugged.

"Yes, come on by. You'd enjoy it," Sofia said.

"You know, my dad orders wine from your estate," Mario said. "He gets a discount from you guys. He really loves your wine. Well, we all do."

"That's great to hear," Nicholas said. "You should visit us. I only vaguely remember one member of our New York relatives. I think it was … I guess your uncle? Giuseppe?"

"Oh, yes, the mobster." Mario grinned.

"What?" Sofia stared at Mario.

He laughed. "Just kidding. It's become his nickname. We only use it among ourselves and behind his back. He must've been a real troublemaker as a young guy. He's a fairly straight arrow now."

"He's Grandpa's and Great-Uncle Angelo's cousin," Nicholas said.

Mario nodded. "I heard you're looking for Angelo. My father mentioned it."

"Well, yes, a few things happened lately that makes it important to find him. Or, at least, find out where he is or was. We don't even know if he's still alive," Nicholas said.

"I doubt we know much." Mario wrinkled his forehead. "But perhaps my parents and Uncle Giuseppe can tell you more. I'm really out of the loop with our … well, let's say, infamous family story." Mario glanced at Sofia with a twinkle in his eye.

She liked Mario. He seemed intelligent and sophisticated. Perhaps Grandpa Martin painted the reputation of the relatives in Staten Island somewhat too bleak.

"Here we are," Mario said. "Good old Rosebank."

"It's lovely here," Sofia said, as they drove through the quaint downtown neighborhood with old-fashioned-looking stores, a few coffee shops, and a furniture store. The houses had a Victorian flair and reminded Sofia a little bit of San Francisco.

"Yes, it's still a nice neighborhood," Mario said. "It's changed quite a bit. Originally, it was mainly an Italian-American community, but a lot of other ethnic groups have moved in since. It's a very mixed batch. I like it."

He stopped the car in a street just one block away from the waterfront and parked it in a driveway before an older two-story home with a yard. They got out of the car and Mario unhooked the gate to the yard. The door to the house opened and a black-and-white dog jumped outside and raced toward them. "Luna," an older man, who appeared in the doorway, called in a sharp voice.

The dog stopped and Mario grabbed it by the collar. "Don't worry. She's friendly."

Luna, apparently a mix between a Labrador and a few other breeds, sniffed Sofia's gently outstretched hand, then let her pet her head. Soon, she wagged her tail.

In the meantime, the man had walked down the few steps from the house and approached them. He was immediately followed by a woman about his age, in her late fifties, Sofia presumed. The man gave a friendly nod and the woman smiled at them.

"My parents, Nino and Rosa," Mario said.

"Well, hi there." Rosa hugged Nicholas. "Look at you. Handsome fellow." She then turned to Sofia. "And your lovely wife. Welcome." Unlike her husband who was tall and slim, she was short and chubby. She had curly black hair and lively, brown eyes. To Sofia, she looked like the quintessential Italian *mamma*.

Nino and Nicholas hugged each other. "It's been a long time," Nino said with a smile. He put his hand on Nicholas's shoulder. "You were a little tike when I saw you last."

"I know, we're all getting older," Nicholas said.

"And welcome to the newest addition of the infamous Segantino clan." Nino embraced Sofia.

Sofia liked Mario's family right away. In fact, she understood Martin's misgivings about them less and less. His feelings for Angelo must have twisted his judgment a little. He seemed to blame the New Yorkers for some of the stuff Angelo did.

Rosa patted her arm. "Let's go inside. We're waiting for Giuseppe and then we'll have lunch.

They stepped into the house, which was fairly large and modestly but tastefully furnished. Some pictures on the wall reminded Sofia of Italy. The house was a block away from the bay. From the balcony of the living room, they were able to see the Verrazano Narrows Bridge and parts of Brooklyn and Manhattan.

"What a view!" Sofia said.

"Yes, the view is one of the perks of living here," Rosa agreed. "I love to sit here in the early morning and watch the fog hover over the bay. Mysterious."

They all stood by the balcony door and watched the scenery. The surface of the water sparkled in the sunlight. Small and large boats were gliding through the bay. Then, barking and a loud voice interrupted the quiet moment. They walked through the living room to the front door. In the yard, a short, plump man was wrestling playfully with Luna.

"Damn beast," he said in a booming voice. He climbed the few steps and came inside.

"Ah," he shouted and pointed at Nicholas. "Our illustrious relatives from the Golden State are here. What an honor." He bowed ceremoniously, then slapped Nicholas on the back.

"You must be Uncle Giuseppe," Nicholas said.

Giuseppe opened his arms. "The one and only."

"This is my wife, Sofia." Nicholas touched Sofia's arm.

Giuseppe's lips curled into a grin. "What in heaven made you marry into this utterly crazy family? What were you thinking? Such a beautiful woman. You could've had anyone."

Sofia opened her mouth, but before she could utter a word, Giuseppe laughed out loud and hugged her. "Don't mind me. Welcome to the family."

Sofia was surprised again at the jovial welcome the New York family gave them.

They sat down to eat a delicious meal of chicken in Marsala sauce, potatoes, zucchini squash, and salad. Nino poured them a glass of red wine and Sofia saw that it was a bottle of their estate wine.

"Only the best for the relatives from the Golden State." Giuseppe raised his glass to Sofia and Nicholas.

"This is an excellent lunch. Thank you. It reminds me of Italy," Sofia said.

"Thanks." Rosa smiled. "We try to keep some of the traditions of our original homeland alive. One of them is the food, although, unfortunately, we Italian Americans are as much into junk food as everyone else."

"Come on, Mom, that's not true. We hardly ever had junk food when I was a kid," Mario protested.

"Well, I try to keep us healthy," his mother said.

"Italy, hmm." Giuseppe faced Sofia and Nicholas. "This reminds me. Martin told me about the skeleton."

"Yes," Nicholas said. "And that brought up the question of Great-Uncle Angelo."

Giuseppe was quiet for a while. "It's a sad chapter in our lives." He got up, fetched his jacket, and pulled an envelope out of its pocket. He gave it to Nicholas.

"That's the last we heard of him."

Chapter 10

The envelope contained a one-page note. Nicholas handed the envelope to Sofia and read the short letter out loud.

Dear Giuseppe, I'm in Italy. Keep it a secret. You can tell Martin and Maria, but please tell them not to come looking for me. I'm fine. Hope everything is okay with you and the family.

"Wow!" Nicholas rubbed his forehead. "Not much, and this is the only sign of life you've had from him?" He glanced at the others. They nodded.

"Yes, and it just arrived a few days before you got here. But look at the postmark." Nino motioned at the envelope Sofia held.

"It was mailed in Italy … in the Piedmont somewhere … but this was what? Eleven years ago." Sofia looked at the others, stunned.

"How is that possible?" Nicholas stared at the envelope Sofia handed him.

"We don't know," Rosa said. "Giuseppe took it to the post office and asked. They claimed that they only received it now."

"No telling where it was held up," Giuseppe added. "Could be in Italy, could be here."

"Gee, what does this mean?" Nicholas wondered. "One thing we know for sure. Eleven years ago, Uncle Angelo was still alive and lived in Italy. Well, it's at least something. Did you tell Grandpa Martin?"

Giuseppe shook his head. "We figured since you were going to be here, we'd give it to you."

Nicholas put the note on the table. "I'll let him know. He really misses Angelo and now with all the suspicions floating around, we need to find him."

"I'm going to be in Italy for a few weeks," Sofia said. "Perhaps, I can find out more. At least, we have the name of the town in the Piedmont. Here it says … Bardonico. I've never heard of it, but my family in Italy may know."

"Hmm, sounds like you're looking for a needle in a haystack," Mario said. "Even if you find the place, it doesn't mean the letter was mailed in the same town where Angelo lived. Since he wanted to be incognito, he may have mailed it from a different place."

"Yes, besides, he may not live there anymore," Giuseppe added.

"Still," Sofia said. "It's better than nothing. This is the first clue. I'm getting excited."

"Just be careful, Sofia," Giuseppe said. "We don't know what happened to Angelo. If he continued his way of life, he may be involved with some questionable or even dangerous characters."

"I hope not," Sofia said. "Anyway, finding an address shouldn't be that dangerous."

"I need to let Grandpa know." Nicholas looked pensively at the note. "Can I keep this?"

Rosa nodded. "Of course. I hope this will have a positive ending."

"I hope so, too," Giuseppe said quietly. "But I'm not convinced."

"Tell me more about Great-Uncle Angelo," Nicholas said eagerly. "How was he when he was here? What do you know about him … and about Grandpa Martin?"

Giuseppe sighed. "It was a difficult time for both of them. And I don't feel proud of the role I played during that time."

"Let's have dessert and coffee first," Rosa suggested. She brought in a homemade chocolate cake and a bowl with whipped cream, while Nino poured the espresso from a sturdy Italian Bialetti pot.

Nicholas took a bite of a large piece of cake. "That's delicious."

"And whipped cream made from scratch," Sofia added.

"Oh, yes, I don't like the one in the can," Rosa said.

They ate in silence for a while. Nicholas finished his cake and coffee fast and was eager to find out more about the history of his relatives.

As if Giuseppe had read his mind, he drank his espresso in one gulp, put the cup down, and wiped his mouth with a napkin. "Well, back to Angelo and Martin."

He put his elbows on the table and folded his hands. "Angelo was a troubled child. I was a kid myself back then, a couple of years older than him. Martin, on the other hand, was studious, quiet, and very serious."

"He still is rather serious," Sofia murmured.

"Hasn't changed much, at least not in that respect," Nicholas said with a chuckle. "But he does have a sense of humor. But go on."

"Yes, serious. Well, he had to grow up too fast. His mother died when he was only eighteen and Angelo was eight. So Martin became a kind of surrogate father and mother for his younger brother."

"Was nobody else helping?" Sofia asked. "That's a big responsibility for a young man."

"Oh, yes, the whole family pitched in from what I remember. There was always an aunt or uncle around. But still, Angelo needed a mother and a father, a firm hand.

Finding Angelo

"Now Angelo had been a difficult boy all along, but when his mother died, he went to pieces. He didn't even know his father because I think he died shortly after Angelo was born and before the family moved to the United States."

"You mentioned you played a role in this you aren't proud of," Nicholas said.

"Yes, well, I was wild and did all kinds of stupid things together with my friends. You know, the kind of stuff that could get you into trouble with the authorities if you get caught. And doing them without getting caught was our goal in life at the time." Giuseppe shrugged. "Nothing major: shoplifting, stealing candy and comics in the store, graffiti, smoking, that kind of thing."

Giuseppe grimaced and ran his hand through his short salt-and-pepper hair. "Trouble was, Angelo admired me. I was the boss of a group of wild kids, and he followed right along. I was not the kind of friend Angelo needed during that vulnerable time in his life. That's what I blame myself for."

"You were a kid yourself," Rosa said.

"Still, I knew better. Anyway, I eventually straightened out, but Angelo ended up in juvie hall for some time."

"And Grandpa?" Nicholas asked.

"Martin went to college and did really well. After college, he worked in an accounting firm. Then all of a sudden, he decided to move to California. He had a friend who'd started a vineyard. Martin felt it would be a fresh beginning for him, and particularly for Angelo."

Rosa brought another round of coffee, and Nino opened a bottle of liquor.

"Grappa anybody?" he asked. Giuseppe nodded while the others shook their head. Nino poured two small glasses.

"I didn't keep in touch with them after they moved," Giuseppe said. "Martin and I weren't on the best of terms. He blamed me for some of the crap Angelo did, and he may have been justified. Later, I heard though that things improved and they did quite well for a while. And then everything went down the tubes again."

"That's when Elvira died, right?" Sofia asked. "We found her diary."

"I think so, yes," Nino said. "And then Angelo disappeared."

"Didn't he come here first after he left California?" Nicholas asked.

"Yes, he stayed with us for about two weeks," Giuseppe said. "He said something bad had happened and he needed to disappear. We tried to find out what it was, but he wouldn't say. He was really shaken up. He asked me if I was still in touch with someone from our family in Italy. I gave him the name of a friend of his father, the only person I still knew of. But I didn't know if the man was still alive. And then, one day Angelo was gone. Didn't leave any message, just a note, saying not to worry about him."

"And now, his friend's skeleton showed up on our property and we're in the middle of this mess." Nicholas smirked. "Thanks, Uncle Angelo."

It was quiet for a while, everybody seemed deep in thought.

Giuseppe cleared his throat. "You know, burying someone's body on one's property is a typical mobster thing."

Nicholas stared at him. "How do you know?"

Giuseppe shrugged. "Read it somewhere."

Nicholas waited for him to go on, but he didn't. Mario glanced at Nicholas, gave a quick smile, and raised his eyebrows.

"How morbid," Rosa said.

Chapter 11

"Do you think Giuseppe knows more about the Mafia than he admitted?" Sofia asked. She and Nicholas were on the ferry back to Manhattan. She gazed with half-closed eyes at the water shimmering in the evening sun. It had warmed up during the day, but the evenings and nights were still rather cold, in the low fifties and high forties. Sofia inhaled the salty smell of the harbor and listened to the sound of the waves breaking against the ferry.

"I wonder," Nicholas mused as they went inside to get out of the nippy weather. "According to Mario, his nickname is 'mobster' after all."

"Yes, and he knew about the bodies buried on the mob's properties. Strange."

"But if that's really true, and the skeleton was buried by some mobster, then that would mean … they're in California. We may be in more trouble than we originally thought." Nicholas stared at Sofia.

"Well, let's not get carried away," Sofia said. "It may just be a coincidence that we found the bones on our property. It doesn't necessarily mean some Mafia guy buried them."

Nicholas shrugged. "One thing is for sure. I'm glad we went to see the Staten Island family. They're a lot nicer than I expected. Too bad Mario had to leave early. I would've liked to pick his brain about Giuseppe some more."

"I'm glad we got that note from Bardonico," Sofia said. "I think it's a sign. It arrived just before I'm leaving for Italy."

"Oh, no, you're not going to play detective, are you?" Nicholas sounded worried. "I hate letting you go by yourself. I'd really like to come along."

"Now, listen." Sofia slapped his arm playfully. "I'm not going to get involved in anything dangerous. But wouldn't it be wonderful if I did find someone who knows something about Uncle Angelo?"

"Yes, of course. But we really don't know what he's involved in, or even if he's still alive. If he does have anything to do with the mob ..." Nicholas hesitated.

"Well, if what Giuseppe said was true, we have to worry about the Mafia in this country," Sofia said. "You going back to California may be more dangerous than me going to Italy. If Angelo had to run away from the mob, he went to Italy because he felt safer there, don't you think?"

"But we don't know if he was running away from the mob," Nicholas said. "He could be one of them. And Italy, after all, is where the Mafia originated."

"He was running away from something," Sofia mused. "He said he had to disappear."

"Whatever you do, please be careful," Nicholas begged.

"Nicholas, please, I'm not a damsel in distress. You don't have to save me. And I'm not an idiot. Of course I won't do anything dangerous."

"I'm just a worried husband. What can I say? Besides, I'd love to come with you, not just because I worry but because I'd like to see the Santuccis again, Julietta and the rest of them. And I'll miss you." He put his arm around Sofia and kissed her. "But I can't really leave the work in the vineyards up to Grandpa. I'll have to be there."

"I know. I'll miss you too, of course. But I'll be only gone for a few weeks. And fortunately, Julietta will be with us this fall. Next time, though, you'll need to come along, too."

The following few days, Sofia and Nicholas did some more sightseeing. They visited the Rockefeller Center in the evening when it was all lit up and watched the people skate on the ice rink that was still open for a couple of days. They strolled through Greenwich Village and took a tour on a bus around the city. They enjoyed the vibrant atmosphere of New York City.

Soon, however, the time of separation came, too fast for both of them. They left on the same day, but Sofia's plane was scheduled to take off earlier. They had a cup of coffee at the airport before Sofia had to go through security. When they said goodbye, Sofia's excitement about seeing Julietta and the Italian family again was tempered by regret about leaving Nicholas behind. A lot had happened the past few weeks, and she would feel better if they could stay together.

They kissed goodbye and Sofia promised to call Nicholas as often as possible. "You be careful, too," she warned him.

"You're telling me?" Nicholas hugged her hard. "Well, enjoy your stay and say hello to everybody … and be—"

"Yes, I'm going to be careful. Please don't worry. And stay away from the mobsters in California."

Nicholas gave a quick grin. They waved at each other. After showing her passport at the customs counter, Sofia looked back, and waved once more. She went through security and walked toward the gate with a heavy heart. She shook her head. *Stop being sentimental. It's going to be fun.*

Chapter 12

Sofia exhaled deeply as she got off the plane in Florence. She hated long-distance plane trips, but at least flying from the East Coast of the United States to Europe was a few hours less than from California. She grabbed her suitcase on the luggage carousel and went outside. Unlike the nippy weather in New York, the temperature here was pleasantly warm and the sun was shining.

She checked the time. It was early morning, so it must be evening the day before in California. Nicholas should still be up. She pulled her cell phone out of her purse to text him.

Just arrived in florence, flight ok, weather perfect, how are u?

A few minutes later, her phone beeped.

Sweetie, so glad to hear from you, everything ok here. Mat picked me up, miss u, love u ***

Miss u too, call u from vignaverde, love ***

Putting her phone away, she looked around and took a deep breath. "Spring in Italy," she murmured. "What a pleasure." She hailed a taxi, which took her to Florence. She was going to meet with Adriano Gori, the lawyer who had taken care of the accounting and finances for her father's vineyards in Vignaverde and now took care of hers. He had been very supportive when she first came here to meet the sister she had known nothing about and to claim her property. They had become good friends.

The first thing she did when she got to the center of the city was walk to a coffee shop and order an espresso. None of the *espressi* she had tried anywhere else could compare with the ones she had tasted in Italy. They served it with a glass of water. After a sip of the fragrant, slightly bitter dark brew, her lips stretched into a smile. *I'm back.* She grabbed her cell phone and called Adriano.

"*Buongiorno*, Sofia." His dark voice sounded pleased. "*Come stai*?" Adriano switched to his fluent but somewhat formal English. They arranged to meet in half an hour.

Sofia walked the short distance to his office in Oltrarno, the older part of Florence. She liked this less touristy neighborhood with its small stores, art galleries, coffee shops, and bars. As she crossed the Arno River, she inhaled the musty scent of the water. The river was a muddy brown. It looked as if it had rained recently.

Adriano's office was on the second floor above a coffee shop and bar. Sofia climbed the stairs and smiled as she remembered his love of strong espresso, preferably with a shot of grappa on the side. She wouldn't be surprised if he had picked the location of his office with his favorite drink in mind.

When she entered, his secretary, an elderly, skinny woman, her gray hair arranged in an elaborate bun on her head, greeted her warmly. "*Signora* Segantino, how are you?" She got up and gave Sofia a quick hug.

"*Grazie, Signora* Amanda … I thought we were on a first-name basis," Sofia said.

"Oh, that's right. *Mi dispiace.* I am sorry. My memory is not as dependable as it used to be." She rolled her eyes. "Besides, you have not been here in a while."

"I know, it's been too long. But we've been really busy in California," Sofia said.

"Well, this is good news, no?" Amanda motioned her to the door of Adriano's office. "Go right ahead. He is waiting for you. Would you like some coffee? Water?"

"I just had an espresso, but, yes, why not? I have to take advantage of the excellent Italian coffee," Sofia said. "And perhaps some water. It's quite warm already."

"Oh, yes, summer is not too far away." Amanda smiled.

Sofia knocked on the door to her lawyer's office and entered. It was a fairly large room with a big window and tons of filing cabinets and bookshelves along the wall.

Adriano peered at her over his reading glasses, then removed them and got up. "Sofia. It's a pleasure to see you again." They hugged briefly. He stepped back and smiled at her. "You look splendid. California and married life must agree with you."

Sofia sat on a chair on the other side of his desk and smiled at his gentlemanly behavior. Adriano was a handsome man in his fifties, a little taller than Sofia, somewhat on the stocky side but well proportioned. He had black hair and lively dark eyes. His olive skin made him look like he spent most of his time at the beach. Sofia knew, of course, that this wasn't true. He was a busy and hardworking man. A year before, he and his German-born wife, Gerda, had taken their first vacation in years on her insistence and visited California. They had stayed with Sofia and Nicholas for a few days. Sofia had fond memories of their time together.

"How are you and your family?" Sofia asked.

"Wonderful." He smiled. "Gerda says hello. Marcello moved to Roma. He got a job as a lawyer there. It's a great opportunity for him. Unfortunately, we don't see as much of him as we would like. But he is happy, so we are happy." He shrugged. "Lucia is still with us though. She is in her last year at the *università*.

"And how is everything in California?" He grabbed a folder from his desk and opened it, then looked up.

"Fine, everybody is healthy. Nicholas sends his regards. We're busy with the vineyards as usual. Well, we do have some problems, actually it's more of a family matter."

"Oh?" Adriano raised a quizzical eyebrow.

"Yes. It's kind of a long story that started twenty years ago." Sofia hesitated. Adriano sat up straight and gave her an encouraging nod. Sofia told him about the disappearance of Nicholas's great-uncle, the hints in his wife's diary that he was in trouble, that there might even be some connection to the Mafia, and the discovery of the bones of his friend in their new field. She also mentioned the postmarked letter from Italy and the fact that she would like to find out more about Angelo's whereabouts.

"Hmm," Adriano murmured after she finished her story. He put his elbows on the desk, folded his hands underneath his chin, and looked at her, seemingly deep in thought. Then he shook his head and grinned. "This is quite a story. Sofia, you seem to attract mysterious and questionable happenings."

Sofia gave an apologetic smile. "It's not me, this time, Adriano."

Adriano's face was serious again. "I just don't know what to tell you. If this great-uncle Angelo is hiding in Italy … the question is, why is he hiding? Has he committed a crime? But you mentioned the diary and the fact that he had witnessed something and that this is the reason he disappeared. So, perhaps, he wasn't the one who committed a crime." Adriano sighed. "But as long as we don't know and, particularly, if you suspect that the Mafia either here or in the US is involved, you have to be very very careful. Just trying to find out his whereabouts could endanger his and your own life." Adriano's voice had become stern. "The mob has no conscience and if they feel threatened, they are able to kill without a second thought. Be very careful, Sofia." He sounded truly worried.

Sofia shook her head. "I wouldn't do anything dangerous. But this whole story affects our family. Our neighbor blames our grandfather, Angelo's older brother, and the police are investigating. Although the skeleton is almost twenty years old and was obviously buried long before we bought the land, still we're involved."

"I understand," Adriano said. "But that is why you should leave the investigation to the police."

Sofia nodded. "You're right. I may just leave it alone. Nicholas and Grandpa Martin are worried about me, too."

"Yes, do not play detective, *Signora* Segantino." Adriano shook his finger at her as if he was scolding her. "But I know you are a determined woman and probably will do what you want to do anyway. Just be very careful. Okay? And if you have any questions or concerns, ask me, please."

"Don't worry, Adriano. I have no intention of jeopardizing my life."

"Good. Well, let's talk about Vignaverde then. The estate has had a few excellent years. You should be satisfied with the proceeds."

They spent the rest of Sofia's visit going over the accounting of the property in Vignaverde. Sofia had inherited two vineyards with Sangiovese and Merlot grapes. She had made her sister's mother, Luisa, and Luisa's brother, Edoardo, who owned the rest of the estate co-owners of her vineyards as well. They did all the work during Sofia's stay in California. They had paid her for their share, and this way, she had alleviated their fears that she was going to sell her property, which would have been a real loss for the family and the estate.

At around noon, Sofia left Adriano's office. She walked to the rental agency nearby where she had reserved a car for her stay in Italy. By now, she knew her way around Florence quite well and wasn't as uptight about driving there as she had been during her first visit. Traffic wasn't too hectic since it was noon and people were having lunch.

Once outside the city borders, Sofia relaxed and enjoyed the beautiful countryside. The high point in spring were the fields full of red poppies and blue cornflowers next to lanes of cypress trees, stone pines, and large stretches of vineyards and olive groves.

After about forty minutes, the impressive Etruscan city walls of Vignaverde, a typical Tuscan hill town, greeted her. She drove past the town toward the estate Podere Francesco Ginori. Soon, the familiar buildings, the winery, cellar and storage sheds appeared around a bend in the highway. She took the narrow road up the hill to the main house, a beautiful stone house with ocher walls and green shutters. When she parked the car in the driveway, the front door opened and Julietta came rushing out. Sofia got out of the car and the two sisters hugged.

"My God, how grown-up you look." Sofia stepped back and looked her sister over. She had last seen her two years before when she visited her and the family a second time.

Julietta looked radiant. She had cut her long wavy chestnut-colored hair that had reached the middle of her back when Sofia had seen her last. Now, it fell to her shoulders in natural curls and waves. It made her look a little more mature. She seemed to have grown a little. They hugged again. A few seconds later, her mother, Luisa, and Donna, Julietta's grandmother, stepped outside. More hugging and greeting in English and Italian.

Luisa had been the girlfriend of Sofia's father. Henry Laverne had fallen in love with her while he was still married to Sofia's mother. The relationship between Henry and Sofia's mother, Cleo, however, had been faltering. Nevertheless, Henry had kept the love affair with Luisa as well as the existence of his Italian daughter a secret. When Sofia found out, she had been in emotional turmoil and shock. It had taken some time before she was able to forgive her father for what she felt was a betrayal. She didn't fault him for his affair but for his having kept it hidden from her for so long.

Sofia went to drop off her luggage at her own house, which was a smaller version of the two-story main house. It stood next to an olive grove and a couple of pine trees. She freshened up a little and joined the others at the main house. In the meantime, Luisa's brother, Edoardo and his wife, Gina, had arrived. They sat down to a late lunch of roasted chicken and a plate of vegetables—tomatoes, eggplant, and peppers— and wine from their Sangiovese and Merlot grapes.

Edoardo poured the wine and toasted Sofia. "One of the best vintages in years," he said.

After dessert and while sipping espresso, Sofia filled them in about her life in California. Julietta showed her the letter of acceptance from Cal Poly in San Luis Obispo, where she planned to study architecture and environmental design.

"She is getting nervous," Luisa said, chuckling.

Julietta sighed. "Yes, I am. Do you think I'll do well?" She put her arm around Sofia.

"Of course, you will. You have excellent grades. I bet you'll do better than the American students," Sofia assured her.

They talked some more and Sofia considered mentioning the story about Angelo, but she was getting tired from the lunch and the wine. She decided to wait. All the family members took a little break after lunch and Sofia went to take a nap.

Later in the evening, before going to sleep, she tried to call Nicholas in California, but couldn't get a hold of him. It was morning in California, the day after they both left New York. He was probably out in the vineyards. She called Martin and Maria. Martin answered the phone. They chatted for a while and Grandpa Martin confirmed that Nicholas was working outside.

"By the way," Martin said. "I just want to warn you again about … you know, being careful with trying to track down Angelo."

"I told you I wasn't going to do anything stupid." Sofia rolled her eyes. Her grandfather was a little too uptight about the whole thing.

"Well, particularly, after what happened to your house. I mean, it may be connected to the whole mess."

Sofia's heart jumped. "What do you mean what happened to our house?"

There was silence at the other end. "Oh, … I guess you haven't talked to Nicholas yet. Oh, dear."

"No. We sent each other a text message right after I arrived in Florence. He didn't mention anything. Why? What's wrong?" Sofia's mouth felt dry.

A sigh. "He probably didn't want to worry you. Everything is okay now. But here's what happened."

Chapter 13

The plane for San Luis Obispo left on time. Nicholas shook his head when the flight attendant presented him with an over-priced unappetizing sandwich. *Flying has become a pain in the butt for more than one reason.* Fortunately, he had bought a sandwich and some fruit in New York and proceeded to eat his small meal.

"Good idea." His neighbor, a young man, pointed at Nicholas's food. "I should've done that. The food on the plane is not worth the money."

"Yes, I learned my lesson on the way over." Nicholas offered him a piece of fruit.

"No, thanks, I'm fine, but I'll do the same next time."

The two talked for a while, then his neighbor began to read a magazine, and Nicholas, who had the window seat, looked outside. The plane's wing sliced through heaps of clouds. Nicholas hoped they wouldn't get caught in a storm, but after a while they rose above the clouds and were surrounded by a pristine blue sky.

Nicholas, however, couldn't settle down. He thought of Sofia with longing and unease. He knew she wasn't reckless, but he couldn't help feeling worried from all the talk about mobsters and Angelo. Surely, though, Sofia knew better than getting herself involved in anything dangerous.

At the San Luis Obispo airport, Nicholas's brother was waiting for him. After hugging each other, Matthew asked him about his visit.

"Great. We spent a few days sightseeing and finally got to meet our infamous relatives who, by the way, seemed a lot more pleasant and together than Grandpa made them out to be."

Matthew laughed. "So, no mobsters in the family, after all?"

"Well, not sure about that. I do have some news about Great-Uncle Angelo. He may be in Italy, at least that's where he was eleven years ago."

"Oh, yes?" Matthew glanced at him with his sharp black eyes, then focused on the road again.

Matthew looked nothing like his older brother. He was short and muscular, had curly brown hair, and his eyes reminded Nicholas of the photo he had seen of Angelo. Matthew had inherited his looks from the Italian side of the Segantino family whereas Nicholas's blond hair came from his grandmother's German side.

"I'll tell you more at home," Nicholas said. The car drove up the hill to their house. "Everything looks fine. Anything new?"

Matthew cleared his throat. "Everything is fine with the vineyards. But I have some bad ... well somewhat unpleasant news."

"Oh, what? Anybody ill?"

"No, nothing like that ... your place was broken into." Matthew stopped the car.

"What?" Nicholas felt his heart speed up. "Oh, shit."

"It's not too bad. Nothing seems to have been stolen. Of course, we're not sure, you'll have to check."

"What happened exactly?" Nicholas got out of the car and stared at the house.

Matthew followed. "Well, it happened three days ago. I went to check on your place and saw it. They forced one of the windows open. Inside was a mess. Some of the drawers had been ripped out. Stuff was lying on the floor. Fortunately, he or they, whoever did it, weren't vandals. They didn't destroy anything." Matthew pulled out a set of keys and handed them to Nicholas. "We had the locks changed."

Nicholas felt faint as he unlocked the door. He walked through the house, checked a drawer in the master bedroom where Sofia kept some jewelry. It was still there. The TV and stereo were undisturbed. He hurried upstairs and looked around the den. He noticed things had been moved, but all the equipment was still there, except for an external hard drive that had been sitting on the desk. Nicholas held his breath, then shook his head. The hard drive was new and they hadn't backed up anything on it yet, and they had both taken their laptops along, so no personal information was stolen. Fortunately, they also had taken along their cameras. They stole the hard drive but nothing else. He opened the filing cabinets and the chest of drawers. Things had definitely been disturbed but at first glance nothing important was missing.

"This is just odd," Nicholas said, returning to the living room. "The hard drive is gone, but all the other valuables are still here. Why didn't they take more?" He let himself fall onto the sofa. "I assume you called the police?"

"Oh, yes, and George Silver as well," Matthew said. "He thinks they may have been scared away before they could steal more. Or they wanted to make it look like a burglary when in fact they broke in because they were searching for something specific."

"What were they looking for?" Nicholas glanced at Matthew. "Perhaps the diary? Elvira's diary?"

"Possibly," Matthew said. "Silver mentioned the diary. Fortunately, we gave it to him beforehand," Matthew said.

Nicholas let his gaze travel around the room. "I'm surprised at how tidy everything is. I was expecting a mess."

"We cleaned things up a little," Matthew said.

"Well, thanks. I really appreciate it." He rubbed his forehead, feeling a headache coming on. "I'm kind of shook up right now."

"You can stay with us or at Grandpa's if you're scared to be alone. But I don't think they'll come back. The window is fixed, and we put safety locks on all the ones on the first floor. You have new locks on the doors as well. You can always have an alarm installed. Or get a gun." Matthew chuckled.

Nicholas shook his head. "I hate those things, both, guns and alarms. No, I'll be okay. I'll unpack and check on Grandpa and Grandma. Everybody okay?"

"Yes, everybody is fine. Okay, then, I'll see you later. If you need anything, just holler."

"Okay, man. Oh, and in case you happen to talk to Sofia, don't mention anything about this. I don't want to scare her."

"My lips are sealed." Matthew made a zipper motion over his mouth.

After Matthew left, Nicholas went slowly through the house again, checking all the rooms. The burglary or whatever it was worried him. It was all clean now, but he still felt violated. They had gone through their personal things. They? Who were they? What did they want? All of a sudden he felt uncomfortable in his own home. He looked at his watch. Sofia was somewhere over the ocean. He missed her and at the same time he was glad she wasn't here. She'd be worried about the break-in. He shook his head, pushing away the unpleasant thoughts. He picked up the keys, locked all the doors, and left.

Martin and Maria welcomed him and insisted he stay for a late dinner. They all talked about the break-in. Martin was convinced they were looking for something and that it had to do with the skeleton and Angelo and the whole mess. Maria brought in some appetizers—olives and pickled mushrooms—and Martin poured them a glass of wine. Nicholas then filled them in on his visit and on the news about Angelo. He showed them the letter that was postmarked eleven years before in the Piedmont.

"Italy?" Martin looked perplexed. "What would he want in Italy? We don't know anybody there anymore, at least not that I'm aware of."

"Giuseppe said he had given him the name of an old friend of you guys' father," Nicholas said.

"Good grief." Martin stared at him. "Our father was a criminal from what my mother told us. He was killed in some mobster brawl. We never found out the details though. Mom didn't want to talk about it. If Angelo got in touch with these kinds of people, then I fear the worst." He scratched his forehead and shook his head, then faced Nicholas.

"About the break-in," he continued. "I talked to George Silver. He promised to have someone keep an eye on your place for a while."

"Maybe it was Frank, the neighbor," Nicholas said.

Martin gave a quick nod. "I thought of that, too. I told him about the diary and that it had revealed that Fred and Angelo worked for the same person and saw something that worried them. He wanted the diary, but I told him I had given it to the police. Who knows, he may not have believed me. I just don't see him breaking in somewhere, though. But perhaps he had someone else do it."

They were quiet for a while, then Maria told them dinner was ready. They sat down and Nicholas smiled when he saw the dish. "My favorite."

Maria had prepared a big plate of spinach and spicy sausage lasagna. With delicious food and wine in his stomach, Nicholas felt more relaxed again.

"By the way, Sofia took the return envelope with the postmark from that town in the Piedmont along. She thought she could make some inquiries while there."

Martin stared at him. "Bad idea. Much too dangerous."

"She's going to be careful. She promised." Martin's reaction stirred Nicholas's own fears again.

His grandfather gave him a stern look. "Tell her to stop snooping. Let the police handle this."

Chapter 14

"Grandpa told me about the break-in." Sofia stood by the open window of her bedroom in Vignaverde, watching the sky color pink and golden as the sun rose above the horizon.

"Yeah, it was quite a shock." Nicholas sighed. He told her that only the hard drive was stolen and that it looked like someone was searching for something.

"The diary?" Sofia mused.

"That's what we think," Nicholas confirmed. "George Silver and the police are informed."

Sofia exhaled deeply. "This is creepy though. I guess I'm glad I wasn't there. I would've gone crazy."

"Tell me about it," Nicholas said. "I could barely sleep the first night. But now, it's okay. Fortunately, they'd cleaned up everything and put things back. Matthew and the family had the door locks changed and window locks installed downstairs. The house is like a fortress now."

"Well, good. But be careful, Nicholas. I hope nothing else happens."

"I hope not either. Anyway, how are *you* doing? How is the family? And Julietta?"

"Everybody is fine. Julietta is getting nervous about going to Cal Poly," Sofia said. "By the way, I told Edoardo and Luisa about Angelo. And Edoardo gave me the address of a friend of the family who happens to live in the Piedmont, a woman by the name of Tina. She lives in a town called Pavone. It might be a lead." She didn't want to tell Nicholas that she was planning to drive there in a few days. She knew he'd be worried.

"Be careful, please. We don't know what Angelo did. All we know is that he's hiding from something or someone." Nicholas sounded alarmed.

Does he suspect I'm planning something? "Well, the danger seems to be at home, not here." Sofia gazed at the sky where the sun had now fully risen. "I didn't get broken into, *you* did. I think I should be worried about you not the other way round. Nobody knows my plans here."

"I'll be careful," Nicholas promised. "Are you going to the Piedmont to see that woman … Tina?"

Sofia didn't want to lie outright. "I may. It's not that far from here."

"But the letter wasn't from there," Nicholas said. "It was from a different town. So why would Tina have any information about Angelo?"

"Oh, not directly," Sofia said. "But knowing the area, she could tell me where the village is and perhaps give me some advice how I could find out more. I don't know. Perhaps, it's a shot in the dark. But it would be a nice outing anyway. I've never been to the Piedmont. And from what Edoardo told me, Pavone is a lovely town and there is a famous and beautiful castle there."

"Okay." Nicholas hesitated. "If you go, you should take someone with you."

"I might," Sofia said. It was a white lie. She was hoping for someone to join her, but she knew that everybody would be busy.

"All right. If you go, please call me every day, okay?" Nicholas seemed to be resigned to her plan.

"I'll try to, but don't forget my cell might not work in every place. But I'll definitely call either you or Vignaverde.

And I'll be very careful not to stir up any mobsters." Sofia laughed.

"Okay, I trust you," Nicholas said.

"By the way, everybody says hello," Sofia said. "They miss you."

"I miss them, too, and I miss you." Nicholas gave a sigh.

"Same here. Lock the house, okay."

"I will, bye sweetie. Call me."

After pressing the disconnect button on her phone, Sofia went down to the kitchen and made a cup of coffee. She took it into the living room, sat on the sofa, and gazed through the window. By now, the fields looked golden and purple and the sun had filled the hills with light and shadows. She thought of her upcoming adventure and began to feel excited. Wouldn't it be great if she actually found Angelo?

Sofia opened the door to the patio and stepped outside. Letting her eyes wander over the meadows nearby, she was overwhelmed by the sight of colorful flowers everywhere. It was the first time she'd been in Tuscany in spring. Whole fields of red poppies and blue cornflowers complemented the vineyards with their symmetrical rows of vines. Even her somewhat dilapidated wooden garden shed, which was partly covered by a wisteria vine, looked regal with its coat of purple flowers. The sweet scent of the patch of freesia in her garden brought a smile to her face. She listened to the sound of birds, greeting the morning. A light breeze kicked up, rustling the leaves on the trees. Although the days were already pleasantly warm, early morning and evenings could still be nippy in April.

At lunchtime, Sofia walked over to the house of the Santucci family. Inside, she was welcomed by a different kind of smell.

It was saffron, which meant her favorite kind of Italian risotto was being prepared. During one of her earlier visits, Luisa had taught her how to make it, and it had become one of her staple foods ever since.

"*Risotto ai funghi*?" Sofia asked Julietta, who was setting the table.

"*Si*," Julietta said. "*Mamma* knows how much you love it."

"I sure do." Sofia opened the door to the kitchen where Luisa and Donna, Julietta's grandmother, were cooking.

"Can I help?" Sofia asked.

Luisa shook her head. "No, it's almost ready." She pointed at a large bowl of salad. "You can carry this inside."

Sofia grabbed the bowl and set it on the table. At that moment, Edoardo and Gina, Luisa's brother and his wife, joined them. Normally, Edoardo and his wife had their meals at their place on the estate. However, the two families, Luisa, Donna, Julietta and Edoardo's family often ate together.

"Where are the children?" Sofia asked Gina. Edoardo and Gina had two children, thirteen-year-old Francesco and ten-year-old Diana.

"They are with friends tonight," she said.

"A sleepover, as you Americans would call it," Edoardo added with a smile. He opened a bottle of estate wine and soon everyone was seated, enjoying Luisa and Donna's excellent meal of risotto with porcini, fish, and vegetables.

After lunch, Donna, who was tired, went upstairs. Julietta, who had some studying to do, said goodbye as well. The rest gathered in the living room, drinking espresso, and talking.

Edoardo took a sip of coffee, then turned to Sofia. "Tell us more about this mysterious *zio* Angelo."

Sofia had given them a few details when she asked them about the town that was mentioned in Angelo's last letter of eleven years ago. She took a deep breath. "It's quite an involved story, but this is what we know." She told them about Martin and Angelo's past, what she and Nicholas had found out from the Segantino family in New York. She mentioned the skeleton, the ongoing investigation, and the fact that they were trying to find Angelo.

Edoardo was quiet for a while. His sharp-featured face, the piercing dark eyes, and the short neatly trimmed beard gave him a serious, almost solemn expression.

"I called Tina," Luisa said, referring to their friend in the Piedmont. "She knows where Bardonico is but doesn't know anybody there."

"Well, it's something," Sofia said. "I could drive there and perhaps I can find out something from the police or someone in a store?"

Edoardo was looking doubtful. "Well, that might be quite difficult. A name of a person from years ago, this is all you have?"

"I also have a photo of Angelo, of course an old one from twenty years ago." Sofia realized how vague this all sounded. "At least, I can try. Probably nothing will come of it, but I wouldn't mind visiting the Piedmont. It must be beautiful, and I've never been there."

"The one thing I don't understand. Why did Angelo come to Italy?" Edoardo asked.

"Well, Martin and Angelo's family was originally from the Piedmont. Their mother brought them to the United States when they were still boys. From what the Segantino family in New York told us, there was an old friend of Angelo and Martin's father still around. Besides, Angelo was hiding from someone in the United States. Perhaps he felt he would be safer in Italy." Sofia lifted her hands and sighed. "We don't really know."

"And you don't know if Angelo killed his friend, the one whose bones you found?" Gina asked.

"We don't believe he did. The diary his wife wrote showed that he and his friend were working for a man and it sounded like it was some kind of illegal work. She mentioned that Angelo and Fred witnessed a crime."

"Then why didn't they go to the police?" Edoardo asked.

"Most likely because the work they did for their boss was illegal and the killer was a powerful man. The police wouldn't have believed them."

Edoardo shook his head. "This sounds more like Italy and its problems with corruption."

"I guess it happens everywhere," Sofia said. "Anyway, Martin is convinced that Angelo isn't a killer."

Edoardo gave a quick smile. "Your grandfather may not believe his younger brother killed someone, but he is not exactly an impartial judge. He is family, after all."

Sofia nodded. Edoardo had experienced his own misguided partiality. A few years ago he misjudged a member of his own family, who brought death and heartache and almost severed the bonds that held the family together.

"Angelo may be innocent and simply afraid of someone," Edoardo continued. "But as long as you don't know for sure, then whatever you plan to do, be very careful."

PART THREE: SLEUTHING IN THE PIEDMONT

Chapter 15

Sofia eased her car onto the freeway from Florence to Bologna on her journey north toward the Piedmont and the Italian-French border. She took a deep breath and tried to relax her tense shoulders somewhat. Sofia was used to the multilane freeways in California, but here she felt insecure in the jungle of signs, the fast-driving Italian cars, and the seemingly never-ending construction sites.

No more gentle hills and fields with colorful wildflowers. Ugly industrial compounds replaced the farms, vineyards, and olive groves.

Another new challenge was the constant toll stations on the freeways and the numerous gates. The first time she approached one, she had no idea which gate to drive through and just followed a line of cars. By accident, it was the right one. There was a serious-looking but polite woman pointing at a box with a slit. Sofia pushed her credit card in, hoping it would work. Fortunately, it did. The barrier opened and Sofia drove on, exhaling deeply. The relief, however, lasted only a moment. A multitude of new freeway signs pointing in all directions confused her again. Luckily, she found the one to Bologna and continued her journey.

Angelo, you better make this worth my while. The next major city past Bologna was Parma, famous for its *prosciutto* by the same name. The farther north Sofia drove, the more relaxing and pleasant the drive was. The view of the Alps was breathtaking. Perhaps one day she'd be able to visit France or Switzerland together with Nicholas.

About four hours later, she saw the exit sign to Ivrea and got off the freeway. After a few wrong turns, she found her way to the town of Pavone and to Tina's place. On the way there, she got a glimpse of the Castello di Pavone, the impressive-looking castle on the hill above the town.

Tina was an elderly woman, short and plump, with gray, curly hair and a friendly smile in her wrinkled face. Sofia liked her right away. She spoke a little English and with Sofia's broken Italian, they were able to communicate quite well. Tina lived in a small house with a beautiful yard full of flowers at the outskirts of Pavone. She suggested they have lunch and then visit the castle. Sofia wanted to invite her to lunch in a restaurant, but Tina had already prepared a pot of minestrone.

While eating the delicious soup, they talked about Sofia's plan to get some information about Angelo. To Sofia's relief, Tina didn't seem to be as worried about the dangers of this investigation as everyone else. She suggested that Sofia go first to the police department, although she didn't think they knew anything, unless Angelo had a criminal record or something bad had happened to him. Others who might be able to help Sofia were the mayor of the town and the priest.

"Priests always know the latest or the earliest gossip," she said, laughing. "I hope you have a warm jacket though. Bardonico is quite high up in the mountains. There may even be some snow."

"Oh, no. I didn't think about that. I only have a lightweight jacket." She looked down at her sneakers. "They're not exactly made for snow either."

Tina shook her head. "I don't think there will be snow on the street, just on the mountains higher up. But there might be a cold wind. You can borrow one of my jackets. She glanced at Sofia's feet. "I also have some thick socks that would help with your feet. You will be driving through here on your way back. Or if not, you can send the clothes back to me from Vignaverde." She went into the next room and brought out a down jacket and two pairs of socks, which Sofia gratefully accepted.

After lunch, Tina and Sofia took a tour through town. Sofia admired the beautiful architecture. Old buildings and modern stores and shops complemented each other.

In the evening, they drove to Castello di Pavone. Pavone, or peacock in English, was the emblem of the town and the castle. The castle dated back to the Middle Ages and had been the seat of kings, cardinals, and other celebrities. It was now a restaurant and a hotel. The family who owned it had done a beautiful job renovating it. Both the inside and outside were left largely intact and renovations had been limited to making everything comfortable with modern amenities. Sofia insisted on treating Tina for dinner. The restaurant was located in a cellar with vaulted ceilings. It looked like an old wine cellar. The food was excellent and they had a nice choice of wines.

Early the following morning, after a light breakfast and a thermos of coffee Tina had prepared for her, Sofia took off from Pavone and headed for the mountains. A narrow, curvy road took her past stunningly beautiful vistas of waterfalls, meadows of blooming wildflowers, and forests. She drove through a few small villages. The higher she got, the sparser the landscape became. Banks of fog hovered over the fields. In the distance, the ever-present high snow-covered mountains greeted her.

It became clear to Sofia why Angelo would choose a remote area such as this to hide. She wondered though how he would survive. Was he able to make a living here? He knew about growing grapes and making wine and the

Piedmont was a famous wine region but up here in the mountains? She had passed many vineyards farther down, but at this higher altitude, cattle and sheep were grazing in the fields. Perhaps he had become a mountain farmer.

When she drove around another one of the many curves, she saw the sign of Bardonico next to the road. It listed the number of inhabitants at 3000 and an elevation of 1300 meters. Sofia realized she was low on gas and stopped at a gas station at the entrance of the town. To Sofia's relief it was a full-service station and she hoped to be able to get some information about the town. A young man stepped out of the small building and filled up her tank. He was tall, lanky, with tousled dark hair and an engaging smile.

Sofia got out of the car to stretch her legs. Now, she was grateful for the thick jacket and the socks. It was cold, the kind of wintry cold that smelled of snow. She asked the young man in Italian if he knew the town well. Since her first visit to Italy, she had taken Italian classes and felt a little more comfortable speaking it. Still, she was relieved that the young man spoke English. They talked for a while and he told her that he learned English in school, and they got some English and American tourists, mainly in the winter for skiing. He liked to practice the language.

Encouraged by his friendly manner, she told him that she was looking for a family member who might have lived in Bardonico about eleven years before. She pulled out the photo of a younger Angelo. "It's an old picture from twenty years ago."

He looked at it intensely, then shook his head. He didn't know of anyone here that resembled the man in the picture. "Perhaps my uncle would know something," he suggested. "He has worked at this station for about thirty years." He motioned her to come with him.

Inside the small gas station building, an older man who resembled the young guy, sat behind the counter. The young man explained to his uncle what Sofia had asked him. She pulled out the photo again and showed it to the older man.

He narrowed his eyes, then said a few words in Italian to his nephew. He looked at Sofia. "Is he a friend of yours?"

Sofia didn't want to tell the whole story, so she just mentioned that he was a family member they had lost touch with. The last they heard of him was a short letter mailed from this town.

Both men looked at the photo again and exchanged a few words in a local Italian dialect. The younger man, whose name was Antonio as Sofia heard the uncle call him, turned to Sofia. "My uncle thinks he looks somewhat familiar, but he doesn't know him and he is not sure. The photo is quite old."

"I know," Sofia said. "Unfortunately, this is all I have of him."

"Perhaps you could ask at the *municipio,* city hall, or at the *polizia*," the uncle said in broken English.

"Yes, I'll try," Sofia said. "Is there a church in town? Perhaps the priest would know."

The two men smiled at Sofia's question. "*Certo*," Antonio said. "Just drive to the center of town and you will see the church. Don Ambrosio lives in the house right next to the church. He may know something."

Sofia thanked them for their help. She walked back to the car with Antonio following her. "If you need anything else, just ask," he said, then waved as she drove away.

As Sofia had read, Bardonico was a ski resort. Surrounded by majestic mountains covered by snow, it was a fairly small town with a few hotels and restaurants. It had a more "northern" feeling than the towns and cities Sofia was familiar with in Tuscany.

She parked her car in a lot next to the city hall. The church nearby was a beautiful medieval building. Sofia found the police station in a side street off the central *piazza,* and she decided to start there.

She entered the gloomy-looking hallway of the rather small building. A few officers in uniform with pistols attached to their belts were standing around, talking to each other and laughing. They measured her with a quizzical look. One of them came up to her, asking if he could help. She told him that she was looking for a family member who may have lived in the town eleven years before. She showed him Angelo's photo. He looked at it, then called the other policemen who all checked out the photo and shook their heads. One of them said something and motioned with his head toward the hallway, which seemed to lead to a few rooms or offices. The policeman who had asked her first, pointed out an office to her and told her to ask the *agente di polizia* there.

Sofia thanked them and walked along the hallway. She felt the officers were following her with their eyes. They were quiet, then laughed and began to talk again. The door to the office they sent her to stood ajar. She knocked gently, then opened the door all the way. A man, reading some kind of magazine, looked up as she entered. He was probably in his fifties, overweight, with a round face, black curly hair, and small piercing eyes. He looked her up and down and Sofia had the distinct feeling he was checking out her body. She began to feel uncomfortable.

"*Mi dispiace,*" she said, then asked if the officer spoke English by any chance.

"Yes, I do." To Sofia's surprise, he gave her a disarming smile.

Relieved she could speak in her native language, she once again told the story she had repeated many times.

He listened carefully, and when she showed him the photo, he glanced at it. His friendly smile turned into a scowl. He stared at the picture for a long time, then raised his eyes and stared at her.

"What did you say his name was?"

Chapter 16

Sofia told the policeman Angelo's name. He glared at her, then at the picture, then back at her. "That is his real name?"

Sofia was surprised at the question and the change of mood in him. She nodded. He looked at the photo some more, then slapped it on his desk.

"I do not know him. No idea," he said in an unfriendly tone.

Sofia had the distinct feeling that he was lying. She took the photo back and waited. He glared at her again, but didn't say anything.

"I'm sorry to have bothered you," she said.

"Why do you want to know where he is?" he barked at her.

She repeated the family connection. A smile curled his lips, but it wasn't a pleasant smile. He shook his head. "I don't know who this is," he repeated.

He made her so uncomfortable that she didn't dare to ask more questions. She thanked him and walked toward the door.

"*Signora,*" he called after her.

She turned around.

"Are you staying in town?" he asked, a little friendlier now, but the friendliness felt fake to her. "Perhaps I can find out a little more if you give me a day or two. Where are you staying?"

Sofia didn't want to give him her whereabouts. She felt too uncomfortable around him. "I'm not staying here," she said.

"There are some nice hotels in town. Come back tomorrow. Perhaps I know more."

"*Grazie*, I'll try to," she said, then left. She realized she was sweating although it was chilly outside.

She took a deep breath. What should she do now? She didn't feel like dealing with any more unfriendly government officials, so she decided to try the priest instead. But first, she wanted to find a place to have lunch. She had seen a coffee shop at the central *piazza*. It was one of those coffee bars that served an array of sandwiches and antipasti as well as coffee and liquors. She ordered a sandwich, water, and coffee and sat down at one of the small tables next to the window. From there, she had a view of the church. At one point, she saw a priest leave the church and walk toward the house next to it. Perhaps he was on his lunch break and this might be the chance to catch him. She quickly finished her lunch, then walked across the *piazza*.

The modest house the priest lived in was built in the same style as the more elaborate church. The walls were made of irregular natural stones and the roof shingles looked like granite. Sofia knocked on the door. It was quiet inside. After she knocked again, she heard footsteps. The door opened and an elderly man with a tonsure of white hair and a round, open face greeted her with a kind smile. Sofia told him that she had a few questions about a relative of hers who might have lived in this town eleven years before.

The priest introduced himself as Don Ambrosio and invited Sofia inside. They entered a sparsely furnished but cozy living room where an electric heater was humming. The warmth radiating from the heater felt good. Sofia sat down and took off her down jacket.

"Would you like a cup of tea? Unfortunately, I don't have any coffee," the priest said in fluent English. Sofia complimented him on his mastery of the language. He told her that he had lived in England for several years.

"Great. My Italian isn't half as good as your English. And yes, a cup of tea would be lovely." Sofia got up. "May I help you?"

The priest's face stretched into a mischievous smile. "Just because I'm a man and a member of the clergy doesn't mean I don't know how to prepare a cup of tea."

"Oh, I didn't mean it that way," Sofia assured him.

"I know. I'm joking. Make yourself comfortable. I shall be right back." Don Ambrosio left the room, and Sofia heard him rattle with dishes. A few moments later, the priest carried a tray with a pot of tea, a small jug of milk, a bowl of sugar, and two cups to the table. He went back to get a plate with cookies.

"I love these." She pointed at the *biscotti*.

"Good. Because this is all I have." Don Ambrosio sat down. "The tea has to steep for a moment."

"Interesting that you drink tea and not espresso," Sofia remarked.

The priest smiled. "I acquired a taste for it when I lived in England." He passed the plate with the cookies to Sofia. "Now, tell me, what can I do for you? You are not from here and from your accent, you are not from England either. America?"

Sofia nodded. "Yes, California."

"Must be beautiful there," the priest said. "But what brought you to this lonely town up here?"

"Well, it's a somewhat complicated story," Sofia said.

The priest lifted his hands with his palms upturned. "I have time."

"May I?" Sofia asked as she held the handle of the teapot.

"You may."

Sofia poured them both a cup. The priest added two spoons of sugar and some milk. Sofia drank hers black.

After taking a sip, Don Ambrosio put the cup down and motioned her to tell her story. Sofia gave him the usual abbreviated version of her reason for being here while the priest listened attentively. She pulled out Angelo's photo and gave it to the priest. He looked at it with narrowed eyes, then grabbed a pair of reading glasses on the small bureau next to him. He examined the photo for quite some time without showing any sign of recognition and Sofia was disappointed, feeling she had come to a dead end.

All of a sudden, Don Ambrosio looked up and faced her. "What did you say his name is?"

Sofia told him.

He looked at the photo again, scratched the bald spot on his head, then said, "It must be him. He looks different here, younger of course. But the name of the man in this photo is Danilo Pedrotti, not Angelo Segantino."

Chapter 17

Sofia looked at the priest, stunned. *Angelo must have changed his name. That's why the policeman acted so strange. He must know him under a different name. Why didn't I think of that before?*

"And you're sure this is the same man?" she asked.

"Pretty sure." Don Ambrosio scanned the picture again. "The same expression in his eyes … how shall I call it? Cautious or distrustful, perhaps?" He continued to look at the photo, then gave it back to Sofia. "You said he's a relative of yours?"

"Yes, through marriage. My husband is his great-nephew and his grandfather, our grandfather, is his older brother." Encouraged by the priest's recognition and kindness, she dared to tell him more of Angelo's troubled past back in California and his mysterious disappearance, the bones they found in their newly acquired property. She mentioned that the police were looking for him, that he might be a witness, even a suspect, but that the family didn't think he was a killer.

Don Ambrosio nodded thoughtfully. "Yes, I knew he was hiding something, that something troubled him. He almost seemed haunted. He never talked about his past. He told me that he was originally from the United States, but I knew nothing of his family. He was a very private person, but friendly and kind. We got along well. We sat together sometimes in the evenings after work, drinking tea or a beer."

"How did you meet him?" Sofia asked.

"He came here one day and asked me if I knew of any kind of work he could do and if I knew of any flats to rent," the priest said. "By chance, my assistant had just left for a different parish, and I needed someone to help with some construction work on the house." The priest motioned toward the ceiling of the room with his hand. "The house needed repairs. So he stayed in the place next door where the former assistant had lived."

"For how long?" Sofia asked.

"Oh, for about four or five years, I think. One day, though, he disappeared overnight. And then I knew that something was definitely wrong."

Sofia's heart beat faster. Finally, some news. "What happened?"

"Well, one night, I woke up and heard loud voices next door where Danilo … or Angelo lived. I was just about to get up when things seemed to quiet down again. The next morning, I went to check to make sure everything was all right. But Danilo was gone, his bags were gone. There was no note or anything. So I assumed his leaving had something to do with the fight I overheard."

"What were they arguing about?" Sofia asked.

"I couldn't understand what they said. I just knew they were having a row. And the other person was a man. That much I heard." He took another sip of tea. "I was disappointed. I liked Dan … I guess I should call him Angelo, since that is his real name. He kept pretty much to himself, didn't socialize much, but he was kind and very helpful. I hoped he would stay. I also thought he had skipped out on the rent he still owed me. But a few days later, I received a brief note from him with the money for the rent. He wrote that something unexpected had happened and that he needed to leave. He apologized for his abrupt departure."

"And that was all?" Sofia asked.

"Yes, I've not heard from him since. I hope that he sorted out whatever was wrong."

Sofia sighed. "Another dead end, I guess. We haven't heard from him either. The last thing was a short letter eleven years ago with the postmark of this town. He sent it to his relatives in New York. That's one of the reasons I'm here. I thought that perhaps someone knew something about him here."

"Ah, yes, postmark ... let me see. I think I still have the note he sent me with the envelope. It's in my desk. I shall be right back."

"Oh good, that would be so helpful." Sofia felt hopeful again. By now, she was determined to find Angelo.

After a while, the priest came back carrying a wrinkled envelope. He held it up with a smile. "Sometimes, it's an advantage being a pack rat. I tend to keep stuff, the little I have." He put his glasses back on and scrutinized the piece of paper. "Ah, yes, I remember." He handed the envelope to Sofia. "It was posted in Moretta. That's a town about two hours southeast of here."

"How do I get there?" Sofia asked.

Don Ambrosio left the room and came back with a map of the region. "It's easy to find." He pointed out the road on the map. "But remember that was several years ago. He may not be there anymore. Or he may have mailed the envelope from a different town."

"I know. It's like finding a needle in a haystack, but I'm here now, so why not try?" Sofia said as she got up. "Thank you very much for all the information. This is really helpful."

"I do hope you find him. But be careful. We don't know the kind of trouble Dan ... I mean Angelo is in." The priest rose as well. "But I can't imagine that he's a murderer."

"We don't think so either," Sofia said. "From the diary of his former wife, we found out that he and his friend witnessed something, a crime, and that's why they left. But still, it's all a big mystery."

"One thing I remember about him," Don Ambrosio said. "He seemed very interested in religion, God, the contemplative life. He asked me what it would take to join a monastery."

Sofia glanced at him surprised. "A monastery?"

"Yes, he was interested in the Benedictine order. I gave him a few books to read about it."

"That's so strange." Sofia gazed out the window, trying to come to grips with the news. "From what I heard, Angelo doesn't seem like the religious type."

"Well, it's not so strange," Don Ambrosio said. "Sometimes people turn to God after a troubled past. Danil—Angelo was searching for something. I'm sure about it."

"Could he have done it?" Sofia asked. "I mean join a monastery?"

The priest shrugged. "It's quite an involved process. You can't just walk into an abbey one day and become a monk. There are different steps and it can take years until you become a full member of an order. But it is possible."

"Wow, I have to digest this," Sofia said.

"Then again, it may have been something he considered and then abandoned. I wouldn't know. I do hope he found peace though, whatever he did. I hope he's all right and that you find him." The priest looked at her with a kind smile.

"But before you leave, let me give you my phone number in case you have more questions or need help." He went to a small chest of drawers, opened it, and pulled out a business card with the name of the church on it. He wrote down his name and phone number and gave the card to Sofia.

"Thank you very much." Sofia put the card in her purse, then asked him for a slip of paper so she could write down her cell phone number. "In case you hear something else about Angelo," she said.

He gave her a piece of paper and she wrote down the number. "I shall certainly let you know if anything new comes up. And if *you* hear anything of him, let me know as well," he said.

They stepped outside and Don Ambrosio accompanied her to the garden gate. "And thank you for the tea and the cookies," Sofia said as they shook hands.

"You're very welcome. It was my pleasure. Where are you staying?"

"I don't know yet. I've seen a couple of hotels on the way here. It's too late to drive back to Pavone today. Tomorrow, I want to try the town you told me about," Sofia said.

"Try Casa Alpina. It's a simple but clean place right nearby." He explained how to get there. "Tell them Don Ambrosio sent you. I usually send guests there. They know me."

"Thank you very much for your help. I really appreciate it." Sofia was moved by the helpfulness of this kind man.

"Good luck to you." The priest lifted his hand to wave goodbye. At the same time, he stared at something behind her with puzzlement. Sofia turned to see what he was looking at. She recognized the man standing across the *piazza*, glaring at them. It was the unfriendly cop. A chill shot down Sofia's back. She hurried to her car and drove away.

Chapter 18

Sofia parked her car in a public parking lot near the hotel the priest had recommended. She was surprised to find a spot. It was spring vacation and the small resort was buzzing with tourists, mostly Italians as she gathered from the people's conversations. She hoped Casa Alpina wasn't totally booked. At least, it was a weekday. The house, perched on a small hill above the street, looked cozy and friendly. It was a two-story wooden chalet with green shutters and a granite roof.

She opened the door and stepped into a small entrance hall where a roaring fire in a large fireplace and a scent of cedar greeted her. An elderly woman stood behind the counter and glanced at her over a pair of reading glasses. Sofia asked if they had a room for the night. "Don Ambrosio recommended you," she added quickly, hoping it would help.

"English?" the woman asked.

"Well, actually American," Sofia said, not sure if the woman was referring to the language or her nationality.

The woman checked her computer, wrinkling her forehead, then looked up. "I have one room left. You're lucky, we're almost all booked. But I can't turn down anybody Don Ambrosio sends."

"Wonderful, thank you," Sofia said. The gentle priest must be quite an authority in this town. She filled out the sign-in sheet while the woman checked her passport, then gave her a key.

The room was on the second floor. Sofia put down her bag and admired the view for a while. The sun began to set behind the majestic snow-covered mountains, coloring them a muted red. She opened the window briefly to air out the room. Outside, it smelled of burning wood, possibly from wood stoves or fireplaces. It cooled off fast and she closed the window again.

Sofia pulled out her cell phone and tried to call Nicholas. There was no reception though, probably due to the high mountains. She tried Julietta to tell her where she was. Fortunately, she was able to get through to her.

"How are you? Have you found *zio* Angelo yet?" Julietta asked her.

"Not yet, but I have a few leads," Sofia said, smiling at Julietta's eager tone. She knew her sister would have loved to take part in her detective work.

"Nicholas called this morning," Julietta said. "He was worried because he had not heard from you."

Sofia rolled her eyes. "I called him two days ago. He's such a worrywart. I tried to call him just now but I can't get through ... Are you still there?" The connection was fading. "Listen, please call him and let him know I'm okay. I'm starting to lose you. I'll try to call him as soon as I can get through."

There was static, but then she heard Julietta's voice again. "Okay, I will let him know. Take care."

Sofia pressed the disconnect button. She had wanted to give Julietta the newest information about Angelo and his change of name, but that would have to wait. She had just put down her phone when it rang again. Perhaps Nicholas was able to get through although she couldn't reach him. She glanced at the number but it was an unknown contact. She answered and was surprised to hear Don Ambrosio's voice.

"Sofia, I just had a strange encounter that I wanted to tell you about. Remember when you left, there was one of the police officers standing across the street, kind of staring at us?"

"Yes, I saw him. Before I came to you, I went to the police to ask about Angelo and I talked to him. He was rude and unfriendly, and I think he was lying when he said he didn't recognize Angelo."

"Well, yes," Don Ambrosio said. "After you left, he came over and asked me about your visit. He wanted to know why you came to see me. I was, of course, surprised, well, rather shocked. I told him that we had a private conversation and I saw no reason to disclose it. Then he became unfriendly and raised his voice and that's when I remembered. I cannot confirm it one hundred percent, but I am pretty sure he was the man with whom Danilo, well Angelo, had a row that night, the night he disappeared. I recognized the voice of his opponent."

"Oh, my God," Sofia said. "That's … well shocking."

"Yes," Don Ambrosio confirmed. "Again, I could be wrong, but I don't think so. And I thought you should know. The way the officer behaved today really gave me a bad feeling about him."

Sofia exhaled deeply. "Thank you for sharing this with me. I felt very uncomfortable around him, too. After he was rude, he all of a sudden said to come back in a couple of days, that he might have some more information. Of course, now, I'm not going to. I better get out of town before he shoots me or something." Sofia chortled, although she wasn't in a laughing mood.

"Yes, I think that's a good idea. No telling what happened between him and Angelo. There are corrupt policemen, that's nothing new," Don Ambrosio said.

The following morning, Sofia left the hotel early to drive to Moretta. It was a cool but sunny day up in the mountains. As she walked to her car in the parking lot, she glanced at a car parked next to hers. It was a Honda Civic, the same brand and color as her car in California, which is why she noticed it. A man sat inside, seemingly waiting for something or someone.

On her way out of town, she stopped for breakfast at a small coffee shop she had seen when she arrived in Bardonico. It was across from the gas station where she had filled up her car on her way into town. Except for a few people, who looked like tourists, the cafeteria was empty. A tired-looking waitress stood behind the counter, then came to the table and brought a menu. There wasn't much of a choice, so Sofia ordered a cup of coffee, a couple of rolls, and a bottle of mineral water for the trip.

Later, as she walked to her car, she stopped, surprised. Parked a few cars away from hers was the blue Honda she'd seen earlier. At least she thought it was the same one, although blue Hondas of that model were no rarity. Sofia checked the inside as she walked by, but the car was empty. Perhaps the driver was in the coffee shop. She tried to remember if she had seen someone come in after her. She shrugged. Must be a coincidence or it wasn't the same car after all. She started her car and eased her way into the street heading out of town. At a cross street where she turned right, she glanced in the rearview mirror. Startled, she noticed the blue Honda again. It was leaving the parking lot, following her.

Chapter 19

"Why would you sell the property without telling me? Frank, you're an idiot, a complete fool."

"It's my property, for Christ's sake. I have the right to sell it to who I want to."

"You promised you'd tell me before you sold anything."

"Anton, I haven't heard from you in over ten years. You showed no interest in the farm. I'm the one who did all the work, who took care of it. And legally, it belongs to me."

"Legally, legally, there was nothing legal about it. My father gave it to you, because he was pissed off at me. I could've contested the will. But I thought we were family. So we work together and not against each other."

"I'm not working against you. You were gone, you didn't care about the property, and so I sold it to my neighbor."

"Great, you sold it to the family of that prick, Angelo. Real smart, asshole."

"Anton, stop insulting me. You've no right. After all, you gave that prick a job."

"Which I regret to this day. Angelo and Fred were a bunch of losers. I tried to help them out, but I had to fire them."

"So what about the bones?" The voice at the other end sounded whiny. Anton Leonardi hated whiny.

"How should I know? I certainly didn't put them there. I wasn't even in California at the time."

"Then who did it? There is an extensive police investigation going on. They're digging, Anton. Both in the field and into the background of the people who are connected to it."

"I don't care, Frank. Let them dig. I've nothing to do with it. Did they dig up the whole field?"

"Yes."

"And they only found Fred's bones?" Anton pulled on his scraggly beard.

"Yes, what else should they've found?" The voice sounded belligerent now. Anton didn't mind belligerent. It was better than whiny. *What a screwed-up family I have.*

"Hell, I don't know. I've always told you Fred was a troublemaker, Fred and that no-good friend of his. Where in the hell is he, anyway? He's probably the one who killed Fred." Anton snorted.

"They're looking for him. Last I heard he may be in Italy, somewhere in the Piedmont. I overheard the neighbors talk about it," Frank said.

"Could you be a little more specific? Piedmont and Italy are fairly big, after all." Anton glanced out the window of his high-rise apartment in Chicago.

"I don't know, some place called Bardonico, I think."

"Bardonico? Well … okay. They'll find him and then they'll have the culprit. So why are you bothering me?" Anton scratched his balding head, thinking hard. *Bardonico, Bardonico, why does that sound familiar?*

"I just wanted you to know. Be careful, Anton. Where are you anyway? … Hey, did you hear me?"

"What? I'm in Chicago. You know that. You have my phone number."

"Where in Chicago? Chicago is fairly big, after all," Frank tried to imitate Anton's voice.

"Shut up. Sarcasm doesn't become you. Chicago is all you need to know. I've business to take care of now." Anton pressed the disconnect button and threw the phone at the sofa in his office. He hit the desk with his fist. "Goddamn it. Stupid idiots."

His wife opened the door. "What's the matter? Who are you screaming at?"

"Nothing's the matter. Now, shut the door. I've work to do," he snapped. He waited until she closed the door. "Nosy bitch."

He stood by the window staring down at Lake Michigan as if the answers to his questions were somewhere in the water. It was early May and the metal-gray surface of the lake glimmered in the diffuse sunlight. "Damn it," he grumbled again, oblivious to the view from his apartment on the sixth floor of a modern high-rise building. He picked the phone off the sofa and, after a brief hesitation, tapped the button of one of the stored numbers.

Someone picked up after the fourth ring. "Yeah?" said a hoarse voice.

"Louie?" Anton said.

Another "Yeah."

"It's Anton Leonardi. We have a problem."

Chapter 20

Sofia kept glancing back while she tried to concentrate on the traffic at the same time. She saw the blue Honda, but then it was gone again. Sofia breathed a sigh of relief. *False alarm.*

Ever since her phone conversation with Don Ambrosio, the uncomfortable feeling around the rude police officer had intensified. Something was wrong there. Why did he want to know what Sofia told the priest and why did he lie to her about not recognizing Angelo? She was convinced he'd lied. Sofia shook her head and exhaled deeply. She kept glancing back but didn't see the blue Honda anymore. After she entered the freeway, traffic increased and she focused on the road.

After two hours, Sofia took the exit to Moretta. She drove along a two-lane road through the countryside. Unlike in the higher mountains, here it was warmer again and the meadows were full of flowers, vineyards, and red and blue flowering trees.

Moretta was a small town, smaller than Bardonico. It reminded her of the less well-known hill towns in Tuscany, except for the snow-covered mountains toward the north. It definitely didn't look like a tourist resort. A few older men and women were strolling through the narrow streets. She passed a school and heard children laughing and playing in the schoolyard. She didn't spot any hotels. In the center of the town, she parked her car next to the post office. She hoped someone there might know something about a present or former resident of the town by the name of Danilo Pedrotti.

The young woman at the counter looked at the photo and shook her head. "He doesn't look familiar, but I have not been here long. Let me ask my supervisor." She waved at an older man, who stepped up to the window and listened to the postal worker. He gave Sofia a stern look, then spoke in broken English.

"*Signora*, we cannot give out private information about a resident." He turned to his employee and said a few words in Italian that sounded like an admonishment.

"He is a relative of my family." Sofia tried again. "We lost touch with him, but he sent this from here." She handed the man the envelope with the Moretta postmark on it.

He looked at it. "That was a long time ago." He shook his head and stepped back, ignoring Sofia. The young woman gave her an apologetic smile.

"Thanks for trying," Sofia said, feeling sorry for her. She hoped she wouldn't get into trouble with her boss. Disappointed, Sofia stepped outside. She looked around, then glanced at the distant mountain chain. She put up her hand to shield her eyes from the sun. *What now?*

"You must be American," a voice said next to her.

Sofia turned her head and looked into the blue eyes of a woman she had noticed standing in line inside the post office. She must have been in her forties or fifties and had short blond hair. Tall and slim, a shopping bag in hand, she looked at Sofia expectantly.

"Yes I am," Sofia said. "You sound American, too. From New York?"

The woman nodded. "Yes, I guess you never lose that accent. I've lived here for several years. What about you?"

"I'm just visiting. I'm from California, but I have some property in Tuscany. So I'm here quite frequently," Sofia explained.

"I'm sorry, but I overheard you asking about a relative of yours in the post office. Danilo Pedrotti, right?" The woman's sharp eyes studied her with intensity.

"Yes." Sofia's heart jumped. "You know him?"

"I used to know him."

"My God, what a coincidence. I almost gave up hope. Do you know where he is?"

"Why don't we go to the coffee shop over there?" The woman pointed at a coffee bar across the street. "We can talk there. By the way, I'm Miriam."

"Sofia. Yes, let's do that." Sofia felt excited. Whenever she was about to lose hope, someone emerged who knew or had met her great-uncle.

"I met Danilo about eight years ago when I first moved here," Miriam said after Sofia explained to her why she was looking for him. She didn't tell her that Angelo had changed his name or what happened in California. She wanted to get to know the woman a little better before revealing possibly damaging information about him.

"We ran into each other at one of the vineyards in the area. I had just moved to Moretta after an ugly divorce. I wanted to get away from everything back home." Miriam tucked a strand of hair behind her ear. "At first, I was quite lonely. I didn't know Italian very well and it took me quite a while to get to know people."

Miriam shrugged. "You know, Italians have the reputation of being very hospitable, but that's only partly true. In small villages and towns such as this one," —she pointed at the old stone houses around the *piazza*—"people can be quite standoffish, even distrustful of foreigners. Anyway, after a while I made some friends and I'm very happy here.

"But back to Danilo. When I got here first, I went on a tour of one of the vineyards in the area. My grandfather had a vineyard in New York State, so I've always been interested in the whole process of winemaking."

"How interesting," Sofia said. "My husband and I and the rest of the family have vineyards in California."

"Yes, Danilo told me that his family owned an estate," Miriam said. "Anyway, he was one of the guides for the English speaking guests at the vineyard. Most of the people in my group were from England and Australia. I was one of the few Americans, and somehow we started talking. After the tour was finished, Danilo had a break and we chatted for a while. He invited me to have lunch at the restaurant on the property. So, that's how it started."

"Did you see him again? How was he?" Sofia wanted to know.

"Yes, we kept seeing each other. It was such a relief to find a fellow countryman here with whom I had many things in common—language, an interest in vineyards, and so on. And he was kind and charming. We became a pair for a while." Miriam gave a wistful smile.

"How was he?" Miriam sighed. "He was very secretive about his personal life. He told me that he had had family trouble back in California, but he didn't want to talk about it. I understood. I felt the same way about my problems back home. We needed to move on, so I didn't push him. But there were other things. He didn't mingle easily with people. He had been in Italy for over ten years, spoke Italian fluently, but he didn't have many friends. He seemed distrustful, as if he had been hurt or betrayed." Miriam's expression was quizzical.

Sofia was trying to decide if she should tell her what happened back home when Miriam continued.

"I asked him a few times, but he said there was nothing. I tried to believe him but ..." Miriam glanced at Sofia, then looked across the *piazza*. "One day, Danilo told me that he was seriously thinking of becoming a Benedictine monk."

"Oh, yes? That's what Don Ambrosio hinted at." Sofia told Miriam about her meeting the priest. "He told me the same thing about him, that he was withdrawn, distrustful, and that he was interested in the religious life."

"Yes, and that was the beginning of the end of our relationship." Miriam lifted her hand, then let it drop into her lap. "I knew then that we had no future together. It wasn't that we ever talked about getting married or anything. He told me that his wife had died and I mentioned my divorce. We were both kind of damaged goods when it came to marriage and relationships. However, I really began to care for him deeply and I thought the feeling was mutual. When he mentioned his thoughts about joining a monastery, I knew that I would not play a role in his future." She paused. "We parted amiably and stayed friends. Until one day, five years ago, when he disappeared without saying goodbye or anything. I was shocked ... and hurt."

It was quiet for a while; both women sipped their coffee. Sofia took a deep breath and told Miriam about the name change.

Miriam stared at her. "Why did he do that?"

"I don't know all of the reasons, but that's what happened and that's why we're trying to find him." Sofia told Miriam about Angelo's past and the fact that he may have been involved in some illegal activities, that he witnessed a crime, that the criminal knew he had seen him, and that this probably is the reason he disappeared and changed his name.

Miriam put her hand on Sofia's arm. "Thank you for telling me. It makes me feel better about his sudden flight. I was hurt that he didn't confide in me. But at least he must have had a reason to disappear." She ran her hand through her hair. "Want another cup of coffee? They have some nice pastries here. My treat." Miriam called the waitress.

"Thank you very much," Sofia said. "If you give me your address or phone number, I can let you know what happens. And, in case you remember something more, here is my cell phone number and email address."

They exchanged contact information and continued to talk, sipping espresso and eating delicious fruit tarts.

"So the last time you saw Angelo was five years ago?" Sofia asked.

Miriam nodded. "Yes."

Sofia sighed. "I don't know what to do next now." She gazed across the plaza. "Do you know if there is a Benedictine monastery nearby? If Angelo was serious about joining, they may know something."

"In fact, there is. It's about five miles from here. Just drive out of town, turn left, and follow the road. It's up on a hill to the right, you can't miss it." Miriam drank the last of her coffee, then glanced at her watch. "Where are you going to stay?"

Sofia shrugged. "Gee, I don't really know. Is there a hotel in this town? I didn't see anything coming in. I also need to get back to Pavone. I'm staying with a friend there."

"It'll take you about an hour and a half from here back to Pavone. But if you want to stay here for the night, you can stay with me. I live five minutes from here."

"That's so nice of you. I really should get back, though. I want to check out the monastery and if I see that it gets too late, I would love to come back to your offer. If that's okay with you?"

"Absolutely. I have no plans tonight. Just give me a call or come by. Here is where I live." Miriam drew a map on her paper napkin and wrote down her phone number. "It's right around the corner, easy to find."

Miriam got up and the two hugged. "It's great to meet a fellow countrywoman. I really hope you find Dan … Angelo. I was heartbroken when he disappeared and I have to admit, I'm still angry at him. But I hope he's okay."

"Yes, I hope so, too," Sofia said. They both went outside. Miriam waved as she walked away. When Sofia approached her car, she was shocked to see a blue Honda again, parked two cars away from her. There was a man in it. He had dark hair, a fleshy face, and scrutinized her with a hostile look. Her heart clenched.

Chapter 21

"You're dead, man."

The guy, his hands tied behind his back, his face bloodied, moaned. "I did what I was told." He was middle-aged, skinny, with greasy brown hair plastered against his skull and falling into his face. He smelled of sweat and fear.

"No, you didn't. I told you to kill them both. You lied to me. One is still alive. Why?" Louie punched the guy's face again.

"Please, I tried. I took care of one. I tried to find the other one, but he was gone." The bound man was trembling, the left eyelid swollen, the eye almost closed.

"Why didn't you tell me? You told me you took care of them, of both of them." Louie raised his fist again.

"Stop, please. I'll do it now. I'll find him."

"Too late. He's gone. Out of the country. Somewhere in Italy. And you're gonna be in a grave soon. If the boss finds out, you're dead meat, buddy."

"Don't tell him. I'll go to Italy. I'll take care of him. I will, promise."

"You're a fucking coward. You're not gonna take care of anybody." Louie slapped the guy again, then untied him.

The man, blood flowing from his nose, stared at Louie, stunned. "You're letting me go?" His voice exuded fear, with a hint of hope.

"Oh, I'm not gonna dirty my hands with you anymore. Someone else is going to do it. Get out." Louie took the guys jacket and tossed it at him. "And don't even try to disappear.

The word is out. They'll find you. I give you a piece of advice, as a friend." Louie smirked. "Write your will … if you still have time."

The man, trembling and barely able to stand up, limped to the door. He opened it and disappeared. Louie turned toward the desk. He sat down in front of a computer monitor. He glanced around the windowless room. Aside from the desk, a lamp, and the computer, the room was empty.

Louie scratched his head and stared at the monitor and his reflection on the screen: a head of disheveled dirty-brown hair, a meaty face, and small glaring eyes. "Goddamn it." With a deep sigh he pulled out his cell phone and punched a button. He recognized the steely voice and the clipped "Yeah?"

"It's Louie. Boss. You're right. We do have a problem."

Chapter 22

Sofia started the car and drove along the narrow street, checking the rearview mirror. So far nobody was following her. She turned left at the crossing and followed the country road that Miriam told her would lead to the monastery. After about half a mile, she glanced at the rearview mirror again and inhaled sharply.

There it was again, the blue Honda. She tightened her hands around the steering wheel. This wasn't a coincidence anymore. She was being followed. Her chest tensed as she tried to decide what to do. She looked toward the horizon where the sun was beginning to sink behind the hills. It would be getting dark soon. There was hardly any traffic on the road, only an occasional car came from the other direction. She was alone with some creep following her.

"Not good, Sofia," she murmured. After a few minutes, she saw what looked like the monastery on the hill, a group of stone houses around a church. It resembled a small hill town.

Another glance back. The blue Honda was closer now, still not right behind her, but too close for comfort. What should she do? Turn back? Drive to Moretta and stay with Miriam? Try again tomorrow early in the day? But she was so close.

With a deep exhalation, she slowed down a little, searching for the road leading up to the monastery. She almost missed it, but turned the steering wheel to the right at the last moment, veered over to the left, tires screeching. She got control of the car again and checked the rearview mirror. The blue Honda passed the exit.

"Got you." Sofia took a few deep breaths, trying to steady her heartbeat, and followed the driveway up the hill.

There was a small parking lot next to a meadow in front of the monastery, almost empty except for a large van that resembled a school bus. Sofia parked her car and sat for a moment, trying to decide if she should have a look around. Just as she was getting ready to open the car door, she gasped. The blue Honda drove into the parking lot from the back of the buildings. *There must be another road to the monastery.*

She started the car, drove down the hill, her heart thudding. She glanced back, but the Honda wasn't following her, not yet. She turned left on the main road that led back to Moretta. She accelerated and drove well past the speed limit, hoping she wouldn't be stopped by a cop. She didn't want another encounter like the one with the unfriendly policeman in Bardonico. Fortunately, there was little traffic and she soon saw the houses of Moretta. She checked her rearview mirror. No Honda.

Sofia drove to Miriam's place. She decided not to park right in front of it, in case her follower would look for her again. She didn't want to let him know where she was. She parked a couple of blocks away, got out, grabbed her overnight bag, and locked the car.

"No." Her breath caught as she saw a blue Honda turn the corner. He'd followed her after all. She hurried down a crossroad to the one where Miriam lived, hoping he hadn't seen her yet. Sweat poured down her back, although it was already cool outside. She turned into the next street and waited a while, constantly glancing around. Perhaps she should wait until it was dark. The sun had gone down and dusk began to spread, coloring the surrounding hills and mountains purple. After a while, she began to shiver, not just out of fear, but because the temperature dropped after sunset.

Finally, she plucked up her courage and walked to the corner of Miriam's street. She looked in both directions. No blue Honda and nobody was out in the street. She slowly walked toward the house, then hesitated. What if he watched her? She might endanger Miriam as well. By now, she was convinced that whoever followed her was dangerous and that his stalking had to do with her trying to find Angelo. Perhaps this sleuthing wasn't such a great idea. She should just call Nicholas, give him all the news, drive back to Vignaverde, and let the police take care of business. What now? Drive back to Pavone? But it was too late in the day for that.

She took another deep breath and walked toward the house. Still no Honda. She opened the gate and entered the small front-yard. No light was visible through the window. She knocked on the door.

"Please, Miriam, be here," she whispered.

Chapter 23

Miriam put the groceries away. She filled the kettle with water and set it on the stove, then dropped two spoonfuls of Earl Grey tea into the pot. Waiting for the water to boil, she glanced out the window at the bougainvillea in her neighbor's yard, its red blossoms quivering in the late afternoon breeze.

She thought about Danilo. She couldn't get used to his real name. The fact that he never told her his name was Angelo made her relationship to him even more questionable. Obviously, he hadn't trusted her enough to tell her.

When the kettle whistled, Miriam poured the boiling water over the tea leaves. While letting the tea steep, she continued to look out the window. A deep sigh escaped her. She shook her head. She had tried to forget Danilo, to let him go, and thought she had succeeded. Meeting his great-niece, however, had reignited the pain that obviously still lodged deep in her heart. Why did he just disappear? Sofia had told her that he was probably hiding from some dangerous people. But still, he could've told her. She wouldn't have betrayed him.

Miriam poured the tea and added milk and sugar. She took the cup into the living room and sat on the sofa, gazing at a small collection of colorful stones on the mantelpiece. She had gathered them on her hikes with Angelo.

She'd been attracted to him because he was different, different from her former husband, a charming, gregarious—and ultimately cruel—man. Danilo was shy, somewhat aloof, often withdrawn, but kind. Her best memories of him were the outings they went on together. They both loved to hike and discover new areas. The woods and mountains around their small village in the Piedmont were the perfect place for exploring. They often hiked for a couple of days and spent the night in some hut. During the cooler seasons, they built a fire, roasted chestnuts and sausages, and sat around after the sun set, simply enjoying the peace and quiet.

It was during those hikes that Miriam felt she got to know him better. He shared some anecdotes about his family back in California. She now remembered him talking about his great nephew, Nicholas, who seemed to have been a favorite of his. Nicholas must be Sofia's husband. Danilo had told her he had been a troubled youngster and he regretted having betrayed his family.

One summer day, at noontime, they sat in the shade of a large Italian stone pine, getting ready to have a picnic. He asked her if she ever thought of moving back to the United States. She was surprised at the question.

"Why? Are you thinking about it?" Miriam asked.

Danilo shrugged. "Sometimes. I like it here. I've been able to live a decent life in Italy. I'm grateful for it. But ... I have unfinished business back home and one day, I have to go back to clear things up. I just don't have the courage yet."

When she asked him to elaborate, however, he withdrew again. "It's family stuff," he said and shook his head.

It was the closest she had come to learning about the problems he had back in California.

That was that. Now, Miriam regretted not having tried to dig deeper. She had been afraid to push him away by asking him stuff he wasn't willing to share. There would be time, she felt. When he was ready.

Well, that time never came. One day, he was gone, without a message. Her heart still contracted at the thought. She shook her head as if to dislodge the painful feelings, got up, and brought her cup and tea pot back into the kitchen. She opened the refrigerator and tried to decide what to have for dinner.

There was a knock at the door.

Sofia stood outside, her overnight bag clutched to her chest, her face pale. "Can I stay with you tonight? I'm being followed."

Chapter 24

Miriam's eyes widened. She stepped aside and motioned for Sofia to enter.

Sofia took a deep breath. "I'm sorry, I didn't mean to scare you."

"No problem. I'm glad you're here." Miriam glanced outside, then closed the door. "What happened?"

Sofia told her about the man in the blue Honda whom she suspected had been following her all the way from Bardonico. It had scared her so badly when she saw him at the monastery again that she just turned back.

"Why don't we both go there tomorrow?" Miriam suggested. "We'll take my car and in case he was really following you, he doesn't know my car."

Sofia was relieved. "You wouldn't mind coming along? That would be great."

"Yes, all this talk about Danilo … I mean Angelo, gee, I wish I could get used to his real name," Miriam said. "Anyway, all this brought up quite a lot of emotions. And I would love to find out what happened to him."

"Good, I could use a helper. This sleuthing is getting a little out of hand," Sofia said.

"Well, Sherlock Holmes, we'll do it together." Miriam chuckled.

"Aye, aye, Dr. Watson." Sofia laughed, then became serious again. "I should really call my husband. I haven't talked to him for a few days. I have trouble getting through on my cell. I know he's worried."

"Call him from my landline," Miriam said and pointed at her phone.

Sofia checked her watch. It was early morning in California and she hoped to get a hold of Nicholas before he started working. He usually went walking through the vineyards together with his grandfather in the mornings. Sofia took a deep breath and dialed the number.

"Hello?" sounded a surprised voice. Sofia realized that he had seen Miriam's number on his display.

"Hi sweetie. It's me," Sofia said.

"Sofia? Where are you? I didn't recognize the number. What's going on? Are you all right?"

"Yes, calm down," Sofia said. "I'm at a friend's place." She told Nicholas that she had received some information about Angelo from a priest in Bardonico and that she was now in Moretta. "I met a friend of Angelo's and I'm staying with her now. Tomorrow, we'll go and check out a monastery nearby."

"A monastery? Why?"

"Yeah, I know. Sounds strange, doesn't it? But both Miriam—that's Angelo's friend—and Don Ambrosio said that Angelo had expressed an interest in religion and the monastic life."

"What? That doesn't sound like the Angelo we know. Are you sure this is the right Angelo?" Nicholas said.

"I'm sure it's him. He may have changed his life around. But the important fact is that until about five years ago, he was still here and alive. So I hope we can get some information from the Benedictine monastery in the area."

"Gee, Sofia, it sounds like you're traveling through the whole of the Piedmont," Nicholas said. "Anyway, I'll let Grandpa and George Silver know. Listen, you be careful, okay. So you're going to the monastery next? Is your friend coming with you?"

"Yes, she knows where it is. And she wants to find Angelo, too." Sofia glanced at Miriam, but her friend was rinsing a few dishes in the kitchen. "They were a couple. And then Angelo disappeared again."

"Well, at least you're not traveling alone. But please, please be careful. If Angelo keeps disappearing, there is something wrong with him. Obviously." Nicholas sounded worried again.

"Please don't worry. We are only going to find out if he had been at the monastery. Chances are, we'll hit a dead end. But I'll let you know."

There was a pause, then Nicholas spoke again. "You know, this all sounds strange. You seem to have no trouble finding information about Angelo but the police here only found out that he renewed his American passport twice. The residence he listed was an address in Milano, but when the police checked it out, an old woman lived there, who didn't know Angelo and had never heard of him. They didn't find any mention of an Angelo Segantino anywhere in Italy that fit his profile."

Sofia swallowed. Now was the time to tell Nicholas about the name change.

"Oh, Sofia, I just realized I need to go. I have a dental appointment. Please keep in touch and let me know what happens ... and be careful."

After Sofia put down the receiver, she took a deep breath. "I should've told him about the name change," she murmured. "Next time for sure." She went into the kitchen where Miriam was chopping zucchini. "Can I help?"

Miriam glanced at her. "No, everything is ready. I'm fixing some vegetables and heated up the leftover chicken casserole."

"Sounds wonderful," Sofia said. She inhaled the delicious scent. "Smells good. Basil?"

"Yes. You can open a bottle of wine if you want to." Miriam pointed at a bottle of red wine on the kitchen counter. "The corkscrew is in the drawer underneath."

Sofia checked the label on the wine. "Ah, Nebbiolo, excellent, the famous wine of the Piedmont."

"Yes, I have it from a vineyard nearby," Miriam said.

They sat down to a dinner of chicken cacciatore and a plate of zucchini, peppers, and eggplant. The meal and the wine relaxed Sofia and for a moment she forgot the fact that not only was she withholding information from her husband, her family, and most likely from the police in California, but she also was being followed by some mysterious guy, probably a criminal.

Chapter 25

The following morning, Sofia and Miriam had a quick breakfast of cereal and coffee before driving to the Benedictine monastery nearby.

The trip in Miriam's Fiat took half an hour. It was a sunny late spring day and Sofia, relaxed after a good night's sleep, was able to enjoy the beautiful landscape. The dark-green meadows took turns with fields of colorful flowers. They passed a few vineyards where the vintners were busy checking and cleaning the vines.

She thought of her vineyard in Vignaverde, her sister Julietta, and the Italian family, working in the fields as were Nicholas and her American family. She missed them. She hadn't been able to talk much with her sister or the Santuccis, and she began to feel guilty for abandoning them. Perhaps after her search for Angelo was over, she could extend her stay for a week to make up for her absence. She yearned to be with Julietta. Fortunately, Julietta would be with her in the fall. Sofia was looking forward to having her sister with her on a more permanent basis.

Sofia, still nervous about being followed, turned around and glanced back, but to her relief, there was no blue Honda anywhere. They came to the sign for the monastery and drove up the hill.

After parking the car, they walked toward the open gate of the monastery. Two monks stepped outside. One of them pointed a key at one of the few cars in the parking lot. The unlock mechanism made a quick beeping sound. Sofia was surprised to see monks drive what looked like a decent car. She had imagined they would walk, use a bicycle, or drive an old battered car. Then again, her education on priests and monks came from TV shows such as Father Brown, which she occasionally watched.

"Let's ask them," Miriam said and waved at the two men. One of them was young, tall, and clean-shaven and the older one had a bushy black-and-gray beard. Both were clothed in the traditional long black habit. Miriam greeted them in Italian and asked if they could speak to the abbot. The two men glanced at each other, then at the women. The older one smiled and told them that this was a monastery—for men.

"I know that," Miriam said, laughing. "I don't want to join. We are looking for a male relative who might have joined the order."

The monks gave them directions to where they would find the abbot, then nodded goodbye and left. Sofia and Miriam entered through the portal of the abbey, which led into a courtyard with a three-span portico. On the right side was a chapel and a small room that looked like a foyer. A monk sat at a desk, reading something. He looked up startled when they entered, then greeted them politely.

Miriam explained the reason for being here. Sofia was glad she didn't have to use her faulty Italian. The monk picked up the phone and pressed a button, then talked to someone, presumably the abbot. He put down the receiver and told them that the abbot would be able to talk to them in about half an hour. He would meet them in the courtyard.

Sofia and Miriam walked around the part of the abbey that was open to visitors. There was a small chapel with natural stone walls and a slate tile roof. The inside was modest but lovingly decorated with a few paintings and frescoes, one of them showing Saint Benedict. A couple of monks sat in the pews, praying silently. The sun shining through the windows lit up the small altar with a simple cross and a black leather-bound book, most likely a prayer book. The slightly musty scent, mixed with incense, added to the peaceful, spiritual atmosphere that permeated the room. After sitting quietly in one of the pews for a while, Sofia and Miriam got up and left.

As they stepped outside, a monk, dressed in the traditional black robe and wearing a cross on a chain, was waiting in front of the chapel.

"I think it's the abbot," Miriam whispered. They walked up to him. "*Padre Abate*?" Miriam asked.

"*Si,*" the man said with a smile. He was slightly taller than Sofia, had broad shoulders and as far as she could tell a substantial body, though it was covered by his black robe. What struck her most, however, were his deep brown eyes in his round face that measured them with an intense but kind expression.

"Do you speak English?" Miriam asked, most likely for Sofia's benefit.

He smiled again. "A little," he said. "How can I help you?" He spoke with a heavy accent.

Sofia told him her usual story, that she was looking for her great-uncle with whom the family had lost touch years ago and that there were indications he might have joined a Benedictine monastery.

The abbot listened attentively, his face kind but serious. He asked them to follow him and led them to the foyer at the entrance where they had been before. The monk guarding the entrance greeted them respectfully. The abbot said a few words to him Sofia didn't understand. She and Miriam followed the abbot to the next room, which looked like an office with a desk and a couple of chairs. The abbot sat behind a desk and motioned Sofia and Miriam to sit in the chairs opposite him. Sofia glanced at the small and almost bare office—it was empty aside from the desk, chairs, and a filing cabinet. There were no pictures or any decorations on the walls. This couldn't be the abbot's regular office, could it? Surely, he had something a little more elegant. After all he was the abbot. Then again, this was monastic life.

When they were seated, the abbot looked at Sofia. "Why is your great-uncle not in touch with you?"

"It's a long story," Sofia said. She had been prepared for questions and decided to be honest but not give away everything. While she talked, the abbot gave her his full attention.

After she stopped, the abbot nodded briefly, looked down at his large hands, folded together on his desk, then lifted his eyes.

"I have a photo of him," Sofia said. She showed him a picture, not the one she had brought with her from California, but a more recent one Miriam had taken of him.

The abbot studied the photo. "You said Danilo Pedrotti is his name?"

Sofia and Miriam glanced at each other, then Sofia nodded, hoping this was the name he would have used in the monastery. There was something in the abbot's eyes, however, a mixture of kindness, strength, and warning, yes warning. *No use lying to me,* they seemed to say.

"That's the name he goes by in Italy, it seems," she said. "His real name is Angelo Segantino."

The abbot didn't act surprised or shocked. "*Bene,*" he said, then faced Sofia and Miriam. "Angelo made a confession." He didn't explain what the confession consisted of.

Sofia's heart pounded in her chest. Joy flooded her. "So you know him?"

"He is an oblate of the Benedictine order," the abbot said. Seeing the clueless expression on her face, he explained. "He is a lay monk. He does not live in the monastery but he attends prayers and mass. He is supposed to live in the spirit of St. Benedict."

"Do you know where he is?" Sofia asked.

"He works in a town about two hours from here, in Rivalta. He also works with youngsters who are troubled. He teaches them sports among other things, soccer mainly."

"Does he live there as well?" Miriam asked.

"I cannot give you his address without consulting with him first. It is a privacy matter. I am sorry." He lifted his hands in an apologetic gesture. "But if you tell me where I can contact you, I will let him know that his family is looking for him. He can get in touch with you."

Sofia was disappointed. She had come so close to finding him. What if he didn't want to get in touch with the family? She took a deep breath. "It's very important that he contacts me or Miriam. We need to find him. The police in the United States are looking for him. He may be a witness in a murder investigation."

The abbot looked at her startled. This was obviously news to him. "I shall talk to him. I shall let him know his family is looking for him, and I shall make sure he contacts you. We cannot have something like this unresolved."

Sofia took a deep breath. "Thank you."

Miriam gave the abbot her address and phone number. They shook hands with the abbot who accompanied them to the gate. Miriam and Sofia got into their car and drove away. When Sofia looked back, she saw the abbot still standing at the gate, a figure in black, guarding the walls of the abbey, this place of peace and tranquility.

Sofia, however, felt less than tranquil and Miriam seemed to be excited as well. "Dan … Angelo, a monk, at least a lay monk. So he went through with it." After a short pause. "Well, then again, in a way it makes sense. He was trying to turn his life around and perhaps religion and the monastery have helped him."

Sofia nodded. "I just hope he will get in touch with us."

"You know, I think I might know where he lives," Miriam said. Sofia looked at her surprised. Miriam's eyes showed a spark of excitement.

Chapter 26

"When Angelo and I were dating, we used to go hiking a lot," Miriam said as she was driving back to Moretta. "One of our favorite hikes was to a cottage near Rivalta where he now works. He mentioned several times that he loved that cottage and would love to rent it. Perhaps he did. Why not find out?"

"I'm all for it," Sofia said.

"Let's do it." Miriam glanced at her watch. "We should wait until tomorrow. It's too late for today. We'll drive to Rivalta tomorrow morning, pack a picnic, and hike up to the cottage. It's a fairly easy hike of about an hour. The scenery is quite beautiful and if we don't find him, at least we'll have a nice outing."

"Sounds perfect. Do you think my shoes are okay for it?" Sofia was wearing athletic shoes.

Miriam glanced at her feet. "They should be fine. It's uphill but not too steep."

"Good, I need the exercise," Sofia said. "I haven't done much walking on this trip."

At Miriam's, Sofia asked herself if she should call Nicholas again and tell him about the latest developments. Since Angelo was known to the monastery under his real name, she didn't even have to tell him about his false Italian name now. She glanced at the phone but then decided to wait until tomorrow evening. Perhaps she would even be able to give him the good news that she had met Angelo, that he was okay. If he was okay. According to the abbot, Angelo was working with young people, helping them. Whatever he had done in the past, he seemed to be on the right path now. But what if his past was a life of crime? What if he had killed his friend? Sofia had never quite believed it.

"What are you thinking about?" Miriam asked. She had started to prepare dinner while Sofia was standing at the window in the kitchen, staring outside.

Sofia shook her head. "Just wondering what's going to happen tomorrow." She turned around. "Let me help you, please."

"You can set the table. The plates and glasses are over there. She pointed at the kitchen cabinet. Sofia took out plates, cutlery, and glasses and put them on the table. Miriam's kitchen had a small dining area, a nook with a table and two benches next to a window. Sofia loved the small house. It was lovingly decorated with all kinds of handicrafts, mainly from Italy. Some of the photos on the mantelpiece above the fireplace were from New York as Miriam explained.

They had a dinner of minestrone and a mixed salad as well as a glass of red wine. After dinner, they relaxed with dessert, a piece of homemade chocolate cake and a cup of espresso.

"You know I think you should put your car in my garage," Miriam suggested. "Get it off the street."

"Good idea," Sofia said. "If you don't mind. But what about your car?"

"It's out in the driveway most of the time anyway. I don't bother putting it in the garage. I'll move it, so you can put yours inside."

Outside, it was dark, and there were just a couple of streetlights on Miriam's street. Sofia walked the two blocks to her car, nervously scanning the darkness. When she arrived at her car, she exhaled deeply, realizing that she had held her breath. No blue Honda or suspicious-looking person, thank

God. She started the car, drove back and parked it in the garage.

"I think the creep is gone," Sofia said. "At least I didn't see anybody."

They went to bed at ten o'clock, wanting to get an early start the following day.

The next morning they got up while it was still dark. After showering and a quick breakfast, they grabbed their backpacks, each filled with a water bottle, sandwiches, fruit, and a lightweight rain jacket in case the weather changed. They loaded the stuff into Miriam's car.

As they were driving away, Miriam noticed Sofia turning around, staring back. "What's the matter?" she asked and glanced through her rearview mirror. At the crossing, she turned right toward the main road leading toward Rivalta.

"Nothing, I think," Sofia said. "I just saw a car and thought it might be the blue Honda, but nobody seems to be after us."

"He must have left. Your car is off the road. Whoever followed you probably thinks you're gone." Miriam glanced once more at her rearview mirror.

"You're probably right." Sofia said.

After about two hours, they saw the sign for Rivalta. The town was small, mainly made up of houses with natural stone walls, a church, a school, and a building that looked like it could be the city hall. Miriam parked the car in the central parking lot.

"Let's have some tea or coffee before we begin the hike," she said. "Mainly to use the restrooms. There won't be one for about an hour, or longer if Angelo is not there."

"Sounds good to me," Sofia motioned at a cafeteria with iron tables and chairs outside. They sat down. A young waiter with tousled hair and sleepy eyes came to their table. He suppressed a yawn and asked for their order. A few minutes later, he brought their cappuccino and croissants.

After the snack and using the restroom, they shouldered their backpacks and walked through the small town. At the edge, a natural path led up the slope through a meadow toward the forest. Before entering the woods, they turned back and admired the view of the town and the mountains in the background. The woods were a mixture of dark and light green trees. In the distance, majestic mountains rose, the tops covered in snow.

"I didn't even realize how beautiful the Piedmont is." Sofia said. "I've been concentrating so much on Tuscany, which is gorgeous of course, but I'm discovering many other beautiful places in Italy."

"Oh, yes. I love Tuscany, too," Miriam agreed. "But I do prefer this somewhat wilder and less touristy landscape here."

"Oh, no, the blue Honda again," Sofia said.

"Where?" Miriam stared at the town below.

"In the parking lot," Sofia whispered. "Let me see … about three cars to the left of ours."

She talked in a normal tone again, probably realizing that people that far away couldn't hear her.

Miriam narrowed her eyes and scanned the parking lot. She saw the blue car but couldn't make out the brand. "It is a blue car, but I don't know if it's a Honda. Could also be a Toyota or … I don't know, Sofia. Are you sure, it's your Honda?"

Sofia shook her head. "No, I'm not sure. I'm probably seeing ghosts. Even if it was a blue Honda, it could be a different one."

"That's what I mean. There are lots of blue Hondas around here. Besides, we are too far away. They can't see us. Let's just go."

Miriam went ahead and Sofia followed. Before they entered the forest, Miriam looked back again. The car seemed to still be there but she didn't see anybody in the parking lot.

There weren't any further scares or surprises during the rest of the hike. They walked mainly in silence, enjoying the beautiful landscape. Miriam thought back to the time she hiked up the hill with Danilo. A feeling of nostalgia filled her. Would they find him? She knew it was a shot in the dark. They knew he worked somewhere in Rivalta but he could be living anywhere. It was probably wishful thinking on her part to find him in his favorite cottage. She tried not to get discouraged.

After a few more turns and a last hike up a steep hill, they stopped and looked back over the valley. Down below was the village, tiny now. They sat on a flat granite plate at the side of the path, sipping water.

"How would Angelo get back to town from here?" Sofia asked.

"There's a road leading up here. It's not very good, lots of potholes. I just thought the hike would be more enjoyable." Miriam gave a wistful smile. "Or I'm simply going down memory lane, since this was our favorite outing."

Sofia laughed and put her arm around her. "It is a beautiful hike. I just hope we find out something."

"We're almost there." Miriam picked up her backpack and began to walk toward the last bend in the road. Once they turned the corner, she stopped. "There it is."

They admired the scenery around them. "Now I know why you guys loved this place," Sofia said.

The cottage, a stone house with walls made of irregular and differently colored stones and with a stone roof, stood next to two pine trees. Behind it was the forest. The house had a small front yard with a vegetable garden. On one side of the cottage, a huge red bougainvillea climbed and hugged the wall, covering half of the roof. An old, somewhat battered car was parked next to the house underneath a birch tree.

"Somebody must live here," Miriam said. "But I don't recognize the car." Disappointment washed over her, but didn't drown all her hope. "He could've bought a different car," she said.

"Well, let's check it out." Sofia began to walk toward the gate.

"Wait." Miriam grabbed her arm. The door to the cottage had opened.

PART FOUR: ANGELO

Chapter 27

A man stepped outside and Sofia inhaled sharply. She recognized the features. He was tall, not as tall as Grandpa Martin, somewhat more solidly built but still trim. His curly hair was almost all white. He sported a short but full gray beard. He wore jeans and a red-and-black checkered work shirt. From where she stood she didn't see his face clearly enough, but he looked about Martin's age, although he was ten years younger. He began to walk toward the car, then looked in their direction, stopped short, and stared at them.

"Danilo?" Miriam said. She began to walk toward him and Sofia followed. "Or should I say, Angelo?"

Angelo continued to stare, his dark sharp eyes narrowed. His face was wrinkled, worn with care and worries, most likely. "Miriam? What are you doing here?"

"Well, hello to you, too," Miriam said, her voice gruff.

The two women had reached the front yard and entered. Angelo was walking toward them, his face one big question mark. He now faced Sofia.

"Hello, Uncle Angelo," she said.

"Who are you?" The tone was friendly, but he measured her with a scowl.

"I am Sofia Segantino, your great-niece by marriage. Nicholas is my husband."

"Nicholas … my God." He looked and scanned the area. "Are you alone?"

They nodded.

"Well you better come inside." Angelo opened the door to the cottage again.

They stepped into a modest, austere but tidy living room. The sitting area in front of a fireplace consisted of a sofa, covered by a patchwork quilt, two easy chairs and a coffee table. On the mantelpiece above the fireplace stood a few framed photos. In another corner was a sturdy-looking dining table with a few chairs. On one of the walls hung a sepia picture of a monk, St. Benedict, perhaps. Through an open door Sofia saw a small kitchen. Another door standing ajar led into what must have been the bedroom.

"Please sit." Angelo pointed at the easy chairs and the sofa. "Would you like something to drink? Coffee or tea?"

"We have some sandwiches for a picnic. May we share them with you?" Sofia asked.

"Thank you, perhaps later." Angelo glanced at Sofia, his eyes more gentle now.

"Coffee sounds good," Miriam said. "And I guess I'll call you Angelo from now on." There was a bitter tone in her voice.

"I'm sorry, Miriam. I didn't mean to lie to you."

"Well, you did lie. You obviously didn't trust me enough to tell me who you really are." Her voice trembled.

Sofia was getting worried that the two would end up having an argument, but Angelo shook his head. "I felt I had no choice. Knowing me, the real me, would've put you in danger as well."

"We always have a choice ... Angelo," Miriam said. "But that can wait. There are more important things now. Sofia came all the way from California to find you."

Angelo faced Sofia. "How is the family? How is Martin ... Maria ... Robert and the rest?"

"They're fine," Sofia assured him. "Everybody is healthy. And they all miss you very much."

"I'll make the coffee while you tell him," Miriam said. "Is that okay?"

Angelo nodded. "The coffee is in the cabinet above the sink. The pot is on the stove. I can make it."

"That's okay. You just listen." Miriam got up and went into the kitchen.

Angelo gave a quick smile as he watched Miriam, then faced Sofia again. "How in heaven did you find me?"

Sofia told him about her and Nicholas's trip to New York and the envelope post-marked in Bardonico. She explained she was traveling to Tuscany anyway and hoped to be able to find something about his whereabouts. "It turned out easier than I expected. I met Don Ambrosio in Bardonico, showed him an old photo of you and he recognized you. But he also said that the man in the picture was a Danilo Pedrotti."

Angelo shook his head. "I knew one day it would catch up with me. How is Don Ambrosio?"

"He's fine. He too wants to know how you are. And he showed me another envelope of a letter you sent him with the rental check. It was mailed in Moretta. So I drove to Moretta and happened to run into Miriam." Sofia lifted her hands. "The rest is history."

"My God, you are quite the detective." Angelo seemed impressed. "But why did you want to find me? Why all of a sudden after twenty years, my family wants to find me?"

"Well, you obviously didn't want to be found. I mean you disappeared and left no forwarding address."

"I did let them know I was okay a few times," Angelo said. "I was in such a mess, I didn't think Martin and the rest of the family wanted anything to do with me anymore. And I can't blame them. But the real reason I disappeared had nothing to do with the family … well, I take that back. It had to do with them. I wanted to protect them." Angelo hesitated. "It's a long story. But still … why now? Why did you want to find me now?"

Miriam came into the room with a pot of coffee and cups. Angelo got up and brought a jug of milk, a bowl of sugar, and a plate with cookies.

Miriam poured the coffee. Angelo took a sip, then set down his cup. "Why now?" He asked again.

Sofia exhaled deeply. "Something happened a few weeks ago." She told him about the bones in the field and the fact that they belonged to his friend, Fred Leonardi.

Angelo paled. He stared at Sofia, then covered his face with his hands. "Damn it," he mumbled.

Was he shocked that they found the evidence after all this time? Was Angelo the killer after all? Or was he upset about his friend's death?

"The bastard killed him." Angelo's voice trembled. He looked up and Sofia saw despair in his eyes.

Chapter 28

"Who? Who killed him?" Sofia whispered.

"I guess there's no use hiding it any longer," Angelo murmured. "Fred and I worked for his cousin, Anton Leonardi. We witnessed him killing another person."

"Anton is the cousin of our neighbor Frank, from whom we bought the property," Sofia explained to Miriam.

"Yes." Angelo brought his hand to his forehead. "Anton and the other guy got into a violent argument and Anton shot him. We got the impression that this other guy was some sort of a rival of Anton, some higher up in a crime syndicate. Anton saw us. He knew we had seen him. We ran away and decided to disappear separately."

"Why not go to the police?" Miriam asked.

"First of all, we knew or at least suspected that what we did was illegal," Angelo said. "We were drivers for this so-called trucking company. I think it was a front for their illegal activities. We transported material from one place to another, handed it over, and waited for the next load. The pay was good, so we didn't ask any questions. I was really messed up at the time.

"But the main reason was we were terrified. Anton is a powerful member of several organizations. We knew that. He is wealthy and influential. Who do you think the cops would've believed? A powerful member of society or two lowlifes like us? And who knows which members of the police were paid off by him."

"But the investigator told us that Anton had been in jail once. They would've known he wasn't the respectable member of society he pretended," Sofia said.

Angelo lifted his shoulders. "That doesn't mean anything. Yes, he was known to not always follow the letter of the law, but as far as I know, he got away with it most of the time. He was in jail for a short time once, got off on good behavior. The fact is, he was and probably still is a powerful person with a lot of friends who are paid off by him."

Miriam shook her head. "But that sounds like some kind of Godfather movie. Surely, the police are not all corrupt."

Angelo narrowed his eyes. "I wish I had your positive attitude toward authorities. Unfortunately, I had some experiences that made me a little more cynical. Anyway, Fred and I decided to lay low for a while. That 'little while' turned into years."

"But twenty years, Angelo? Why did you never contact the family?" Sofia asked.

"I didn't want to involve them. I was afraid they were going to try to find us. The farther away I was from the family, the less they were affected. At least that's what I hoped." He hesitated. "Also, I was ashamed. Martin had helped me out so many times, and I betrayed him again and again. And then my wife died and it was my fault, really. I was on my last leg. I had enough money saved up to live for a while. I wanted to get away as far as possible from everything." His voice sounded hoarse.

It was quiet for a while. Angelo sat bent over staring at the floor.

"Why don't we eat something. This is going to be a long confession." Miriam put her hand on Angelo's shoulder. "We need some sustenance."

"Good idea," Angelo said.

Sofia unpacked the sandwiches and Miriam brought some plates from the kitchen. Angelo got up and slowly walked into the kitchen, slightly hunched over. He seemed to have aged in the last ten minutes. He came back with glasses and a jug of water and three bottles of lemonade. "That's all I have." He put the bottles on the table.

"I love those." Sofia pointed at the lemonade. "But I'm fine with water. I don't want to drink you out of house and home."

Angelo shook his head. "No problem. There are grocery stores in town. I can get more. I just didn't expect any visitors."

They ate in silence. Angelo nibbled on his sandwich but didn't seem very hungry. Sofia had time to observe him more carefully. She still saw Grandpa Martin in his features, but there was something else. Whereas Martin had soft brown eyes, Angelo's eyes were almost black and piercing. His demeanor was quiet, withdrawn, and serious. Martin was serious as well but had a dry sense of humor. Angelo seemed to lack that kind of humor, at least Sofia hadn't seen any evidence of it. Then again, there hadn't been much of a chance for humor.

They finished their sandwich and Angelo asked if they wanted more coffee. "I'll make some. Just relax," Miriam said.

Sofia wondered how well Miriam was holding up. She must be devastated by Angelo's confession and the fact that he had withheld all this from her.

"What made you decide to live in Italy?" Sofia asked him.

Angelo took a sip of water and looked down at his hands. He turned them over and checked his palms. "I wanted to see if I could find someone on my father's side. Our father died when I was three. My whole life I've wanted to find out more about him. Giuseppe in New York gave me the address of a friend of my father who was still alive. This man, he's dead now, helped me out in the beginning. He provided me with a false identity, papers, and all that." Angelo chortled. "Obviously, I was not the only one who lived a less than honorable life and skirted the law."

"The investigator told us that they found out that you renewed your American passport twice, under your real name obviously," Sofia said.

Angelo nodded. "Yes, in the back of my mind I always wanted to return one day. I love Italy and the few friends I made here. They gave me the opportunity to turn my life around. But I often missed my family, my country. I felt bad for abandoning them."

"You know they're looking for you in California," Sofia said. "Ever since they found the skeleton in our field."

"Am I a suspect in his murder?" Angelo asked. He didn't sound worried or shocked.

"The last I heard they want you for questioning," Sofia said. "By the way, they don't know you're here under a false name. They may suspect it, but they wouldn't know your fake name … I haven't told anyone."

Angelo looked at her surprised. "Why not? You're withholding pertinent information."

Sofia raised an eyebrow. "Not as pertinent as your information of twenty years ago about a murder."

"I guess so." His eyes showed a humorous spark. So he had a sense of humor, too, just like his brother. "You should tell them. Well, actually, I need to tell them. I need to go back. I need to help the police clear this up and I need to clear my name. I just have to take care of a few things beforehand. I need to inform the abbot at Novalesa, and I need to find someone to take over my classes. I can't just abandon the kids."

"Would there be someone who could fill in for you?" Miriam asked. She'd been very quiet the whole time, but she seemed composed.

"I have someone in mind. We take turns, and he is very good and the children like him."

"If you need help while you're away, let me know," Miriam said matter-of-factly.

Angelo turned to her. "Thank you. Perhaps check on the cabin occasionally? You could use it for vacation."

"I wouldn't mind checking on the cottage. But staying here? No, it would be too painful. It would remind me of the good times we had together, before you just up and left." Now, Miriam sounded bitter.

Angelo lowered his gaze. "I'm really sorry, Miriam."

"Well, you should be."

Sofia felt the two should have some private time. She got up. "Would you mind if I looked around outside? It's such a gorgeous place."

"Go ahead," Angelo said. "There is a short path to the left of the cabin. It leads to a pond. Very pretty. Just don't wander off too far."

"I won't. I'll see you in a while." Miriam gave her a weak smile that seemed to say "thank you." Sofia went outside and took a deep breath. It had cooled off a little, and in the sky behind the forest, heaps of dark clouds were forming.

Sofia walked along the path through a forest of mainly light-green birches and a few stone pines. There was the sound of a spring and after about two hundred yards, the woods opened onto a meadow and a small pond bordered by reeds and bushes. It smelled of moss and some kind of herb she didn't recognize. She sat down on a rock next to the pond and listened to a concert of birds tweeting all around her.

Chapter 29

An uncomfortable silence permeated the room after Sofia had left. Angelo tried to find the right words to ease the hurt he had inflicted on yet another person. He liked Miriam a lot, even loved her, and had felt guilty for disappearing. He had seen the guy again, the same one who had chased him out of Bardonico. They had been friends once, but the friendship had soured when Angelo discovered his true character and intent. A few years later, the man showed up in Moretta as well and Angelo panicked. He had to disentangle himself from people he was close to once again, because he feared putting them in harm's way.

"I know you hate me for just disappearing, and I don't blame you. But I can only say I had legitimate reasons to do it."

"I don't hate you. I know now that you needed to hide, to hide from your enemies and perhaps also from your old life. You needed a sanctuary. What I don't understand is why you didn't tell me. We were together for two years. You knew me. Why didn't you trust me?"

"It wasn't distrust. I just didn't want you to know things that could've put you in danger. The people I'm running from are lethal. They don't care about human life and if they feel just the slightest bit threatened, they don't hesitate to kill. I already lost my wife to my way of life. I didn't want to cause anyone else's death." Angelo felt a knot in his throat. "Now I know that I lost Fred as well."

"He wasn't your responsibility. Didn't you say he was the one who introduced you to his cousin? He knew the danger. It could've been the other way round. You could be dead and he could've survived."

"True, but I am the one who is still hunted and anybody with me is in danger as well."

"Isn't that a little exaggerated?"

"No, it isn't."

"Whatever. Things are the way they are. I just hope you'll be able to resolve all this and finally find peace."

"I hope so, too. I was a coward, Miriam. I guess what I said is only halfway true. I tried not to endanger other people. But if that had been the only reason all along, I would've gone to the police when I witnessed the killing. I would've accepted the consequences. Instead, I ran away and I've been on the run ever since."

Angelo covered his face with his hands. He was so weary and tired. He looked up as he felt a hand on his shoulder. He took Miriam's hand and kissed it. "I guess all this talk doesn't change anything. All I can say again is I'm sorry."

"It's okay. You know the most important thing is to forgive yourself. I know you're not a bad person. You've made mistakes in your life, but you've never given up. Perhaps came close, but you've always found a way to go on. You're doing something worthwhile. You help youngsters, young people in trouble, as you yourself were once. Don't give up now."

Angelo's eyes filled with tears. He hugged Miriam. "Thanks."

They heard the garden gate squeak. Angelo looked up and wiped his eyes. "Nicholas sure got himself a beautiful wife. Not just beautiful, but smart. I still don't know how she was able to track me down. I guess you're responsible for that, too."

"She did most of the detective work. The abbot at the Abbey of Novalesa didn't want to give us your address. He told us where you worked. But the rest was private information. We told him it was important to get a hold of you, so he said he would contact you. But then I remembered the cottage and our favorite hike. So we decided to give it a try."

The door opened. "Well, hello, Sherlock Holmes," Miriam said.

Sofia grinned. "Hi, Dr. Watson."

Angelo shook his head. "You two are something else."

"I think it's going to rain. I wonder if we should leave now. Otherwise, we won't make it to town before the storm," Sofia said.

"I can drive you." Angelo got up and checked his watch, then stepped outside and scanned the sky. It began to rain and within a few minutes, the rain turned into a torrential downpour. Angelo scratched his head. "It may be too late. You ladies may have to spend the night. Once it rains like this, the road washes out. It would be too dangerous to drive."

Miriam and Sofia looked at each other. "But we can't just stay here, can we?" Sofia asked.

"Do you have to be somewhere tonight?" Angelo asked.

Both women shook their head. "Our car is parked in a public lot. Do you think it'll be okay overnight?" Sofia asked.

"That shouldn't be a problem," Miriam said.

"Okay, why don't you stay? It's rare that I have company. I can drive you to town tomorrow morning."

Sofia looked around. "Where would we sleep?"

"In my bed. It's not huge but big enough for two slender ladies." Angelo opened the door to the bedroom. "I'll sleep on the sofa. It's very comfortable. Really."

Miriam glanced at Sofia. "What do you think?"

"It's okay, yes. If you don't mind." Sofia looked at Angelo with her purple-blue eyes. He was struck once again how much he had missed being away for twenty years. He smiled.

"What?" Sofia asked.

Angelo shook his head. "I just can't get it into my head. The last time I saw Nicholas he was … what? … eight or nine years old, and now he's married." He walked into the bedroom. "Let me give you some clean sheets and towels."

"Okay, what about dinner?" Miriam asked.

Angelo turned around. "I have enough for a simple meal. And I think I even have some wine."

"Good, but we'll prepare dinner," Sofia said.

"If you insist." Angelo pulled the sheets from his bed, grabbed clean ones in the chest of drawers. He looked outside. The rain came down hard now. It pelted the windows and the walls and drummed on the stone roof.

Just as he turned away he thought he saw movement at the edge of the forest, a shape that didn't belong there. But when he stepped closer, it was gone. He narrowed his eyes and watched for a while. Nothing. He turned around and laid the clean sheets, pillow cases, a comforter, and towels on the bed.

"I also have to let Martin and the others know that we found you," Sofia said. "They're really worried about my sleuthing and of course they're worried about you, Uncle Angelo."

"You may have to wait until tomorrow," Angelo said. "I don't have a landline and the cell phone only works intermittently and probably not with this storm."

"Okay, well, one day more or less won't make much difference anyway."

Chapter 30

Sofia and Miriam were in the kitchen preparing dinner. They found a package of spaghetti and a jar of tomato sauce in the kitchen cabinet. There was lettuce, cucumbers, olives, and tomatoes in the fridge as well as a hunk of Parmesan cheese. Angelo opened a bottle of red wine.

"This is going to be a real party," Sofia said. Angelo smiled at her and she noticed again the furrows and grooves of care and pain in his face. Some of the lines were caused by laughter, though. So he hadn't forgotten that part of his being.

"What are we celebrating?" he asked.

"Finding Angelo?" Sofia suggested.

"I'll drink to that," Miriam said.

"Not sure how that's going to affect my life, but I guess I'll drink to it, too." Angelo poured three glasses of wine.

They had a simple dinner of pasta, salad, and wine. After the meal, they sat in the living room, drinking espresso. Outside, the storm had subsided and given way to a more gentle downpour. In the house, there was a scent of tomato sauce and coffee. Sofia felt relaxed and content. It began to dawn on her that she'd actually found her and Nicholas's great-uncle and Martin's long-lost younger brother. What an adventure it had been. She sipped her coffee and faced Angelo.

"Tell me about your time in Italy. How did you get here? What happened?"

Angelo rubbed his beard and exhaled deeply. "It's a long story."

"We have time," Sofia said.

Angelo put his cup down and held his hands folded in his lap. "After I left California, I spent some time with Giuseppe, Nino and his wife in New York."

Sofia nodded. "Yes, Nicholas and I went to see them and they told me about that. They also showed me an envelope of a letter you sent them eleven years ago. Somehow it got lost in the mail and they received it a short time before we went to visit them. It was post-marked in Bardonico."

Angelo gave her an inquiring look. "Is that what made you come to Italy?"

"Well, not really. I was supposed to come here anyway, to visit my sister in Tuscany and look after my vineyards there. But yes I decided to make some inquiries."

A look of surprise flashed over Angelo's face. "You have a sister and vineyards in Tuscany?"

"Yes, that's where I met Nicholas. But that's another long story. I want to know more about you now. I think I deserve it after having tracked you down."

Angelo gave a quick smile. "Okay, as I mentioned, Giuseppe gave me an address of a friend of my father in the Piedmont. I had some savings, so I bought a plane ticket and left. The guy, a very old man by then—he died a couple of years later—arranged for some fake documentation for me."

"That's how you became Danilo Pedrotti?" Miriam asked.

"Yes. I was afraid that Anton was going to try to track me down. The first five years, I lived in different places in the Piedmont, doing mainly seasonal work. Then someone I worked for told me about a place in the mountains where I might be able to get more steady work. Since it was a tourist resort and I spoke English, I might be able to find a job as a tour guide or something similar. He also knew someone who lived in Bardonico and might be able to help me get work.

Anyway, I thought I'd give it a try. As it turned out, there wasn't anything of that sort available. There weren't enough English-speaking tourists. Fortunately though, I found Don Ambrosio, who needed an assistant."

"The priest whom I met as well," Sofia added.

"Yes. And he was one of the people who truly helped me turn my life around. He asked me to help around the church and became something like a mentor to me. I've never considered myself religious." Angelo scratched his beard. "And with the life I've led, I certainly didn't think that God looked kindly on me. Don Ambrosio helped me realize that I could always start new, that God would forgive me if I truly repented."

"Is that when you decided to become a monk?" Sofia asked.

"Well, no, not right away. I wasn't ready for a truly religious life. But being around him and watching him, the way he always helped someone in need without making a big deal out of it. How he lived a simple life, worked hard without much compensation. It made a big impression on me. See, since childhood I've shunned responsibility. I wanted things without working for them. But when I came to Italy, all I wanted was peace. I longed for peace, and sitting with Don Ambrosio in that chapel, I found it … at least for a while."

"And then what happened?" Miriam asked.

"In Bardonico, I met Fabio, the acquaintance of my former employer, and we became friends. Not close friends. I was somewhat leery of him. I sensed something not quite right. But before I met Don Ambrosio, I was pretty lonely." He shrugged. "So anybody who would share a beer and a chat with me was better than spending all my time after work in my tiny room. Once I began working for Don Ambrosio, he let me stay in an apartment next to the church. I also got busy, and so Fabio and I didn't hang out that much anymore. Besides, he got promoted in the police department."

"Police department?" Sofia asked. "Was he a cop?"

Angelo nodded. "Yes."

Sofia opened her mouth, then closed it again. Her head was spinning. "Oh, my God."

"What?" Angelo scrutinized her.

"Was he the man you had an argument with and then left the following day?"

Angelo stared at her. "Yes. How do you know that?"

"Darn." Sofia put her hand on her forehead. She tried to figure out what this meant. "When I met Don Ambrosio ... well, before I met him, when I first came to Bardonico, I went to the police department."

"Why?" Angelo glared at her.

"Well, the only information I had was the letter from Bardonico. I figured if you stayed there for some time, perhaps the police would know."

"Okay." Angelo's voice was guarded.

"The officers sent me to a higher-up. I asked him about you and showed him an old photo of you."

Angelo groaned. "Let me guess. You told him my real name."

Sofia nodded. "I'm sorry, I didn't know."

"It's okay. Go on." Angelo fixed her with his black eyes."

"He claimed not to know you, but he was hostile, and I had the feeling he was lying."

"Oh, yes. He knew then that I was using a fake name," Angelo said quietly. "But how did you know about the argument?"

Sofia told him about Don Ambrosio's phone call to her, that the policeman had seen her go to the priest and that he wanted to know what they talked about. "He yelled at Don

Ambrosio, and the priest recognized the voice from the argument you had the night before you disappeared."

Angelo closed his eyes and lifted his hand to his forehead, rubbing it.

"I'm sorry, Uncle Angelo," Sofia said.

"It's okay," he said after a short pause. "You didn't know. I knew it would come out one day. It just means, it's even more urgent now that I leave and somehow return to California. I'm not safe here anymore."

"But why? So the cop knows that you used a fake name. But you're gone. He doesn't know where you are," Miriam said.

"He is determined to find me, and eventually he will. The pieces of the puzzle are beginning to fall into place," Angelo muttered.

"What pieces of the puzzle?" Miriam asked.

Chapter 31

Angelo got up and walked to the window. He sat on the window ledge, and faced Sofia and Miriam.

"Fabio—the policeman you talked to—came by one day and made me an offer. He told me he was working for a man in the United States who imported small but precious art objects from Italy. They were looking for someone who would take them on the plane and hand them over at the airport in Chicago. Someone would meet me there, and I would deliver the goods to him. Payment was generous and included a round trip plane ticket and a night in a hotel near the airport."

Angelo sneered. "The whole thing sounded fishy, of course, and reminded me of the illegal transportation deals Fred and I made in California. I asked Fabio why he didn't do it himself. He told me they needed a trustworthy American citizen who could fly in and out of the United States undetected. I told him I would need to know who I was dealing with in the United States, that this sounded dangerous and illegal. He said he didn't know who the person was. He knew only that his employer was someone in Chicago. The person who'd offered him the job referred to the man as Cricket. Now, I knew who I was dealing with. Cricket was the code name for Anton Leonardi."

"Fred and Frank Leonardi's cousin," Sofia said.

Angelo nodded. "Yes. I warned Fabio, told him I knew the man in Chicago, that he was a dangerous criminal and that Fabio should stay away from him. Fabio at first seemed shocked and said he was going to check it out. I hoped he would come to his senses. See, Fabio is one of those underpaid Italian policemen. He constantly complained about the working conditions. He had a family to support, and I understood that he was tempted by easy money. I also knew what can happen if you get involved in such illegal crap."

Angelo sighed. "I now wish I hadn't warned him and just refused the offer, because what followed forced me to disappear again. A few days later, Fabio came back and confronted me, saying that he had trusted me and now he regretted having told me anything.

"I told him I wasn't going to betray him. As far as I was concerned, he'd made me an offer and I had turned it down. The rest was up to him. But I warned him again that Cricket or Anton Leonardi was not to be trifled with. Then he yelled at me and said that he knew I was hiding here. His contact to Cricket, the one who had offered him the job, would be able to find out why I was on the run. Unfortunately, I had hinted at the fact that I'd had some trouble back home, but I hadn't told him what it was.

"However, I realized that if Anton found out that somebody from California was hiding in Italy, he may very well put two and two together. He was too close, so I panicked and left."

"And when I showed him your photo and told him your real name, that made him even more suspicious. I'm so sorry," Sofia said.

"Well, you didn't know and fortunately, I had disappeared before he found out."

"But why did you disappear when you lived in Moretta?" Miriam asked.

"I began receiving anonymous and threatening letters," Angelo said. "I also saw Fabio once in Moretta. I suspected right away that he was the one who sent the letters."

Angelo walked over to the sofa and sat down. "The letters also contained veiled threats, suggesting that my close friends were in danger. At that point, I thought about going to the authorities, finally. But which ones? Fabio was with the police after all." He exhaled deeply. "So I ran again."

It was quiet in the room, then Miriam got up. "What a mess." She sat next to Angelo and put her hand on his. Then she got up. "I just thought of something. What about the blue Honda?"

"Blue Honda? What blue Honda?" Angelo asked.

"Oh, yes. I think I was being followed when I left Bardonico for Moretta," Sofia said. "A blue Honda kept parking close to my car. At first I thought nothing of it. There are tons of blue Hondas, but after a while, I became suspicious. Do you know if the police officer, this Fabio, has a blue Honda?"

Angelo shook his head. "No. I don't. But I've been gone for a while. It's possible. For how long did you think you were being followed?"

Sofia and Miriam looked at each other. "When I first tried to check out the abbey, I saw the car and he followed me to the monastery. I panicked and turned back and on the way back I must have lost him. From then on we used Miriam's car. My car is hidden in her garage."

Angelo's eyes narrowed. "How did you know it was a man?"

"I saw him once, just for a brief moment. I know it wasn't the policeman. It was someone else," Sofia said.

"Well, Fabio could've sent someone else to follow you. He wouldn't necessarily do it himself." Angelo looked pensive.

"Once he knew what my real name was and he happened to mention it to the go-between, the man who offered him the job, then Anton may have found out that I was in Italy."

"We thought for a quick moment that a blue Honda was parked at the public lot in Rivalta, when we left for the hike. But we really didn't know. It could've been a coincidence. And I'm sure we weren't followed on the hike," Miriam said.

"Well, this is all very disturbing. Tomorrow I'm going to pack a bag, take my passport, and leave. I'll have to let Abbot Francesco know. Perhaps I can stay at the abbey for a few days until I have the airplane ticket."

"Why don't you come with me to Tuscany?" Sofia suggested. "From there we can call California, the family, and let George Silver know that you want to come back. There is plenty of room at my place and the cop certainly wouldn't know you're there."

Angelo watched her, thinking. "I just don't want to get someone else in danger. Your family in Tuscany, for instance."

"That won't happen. We won't stay there very long. You need to get back, so all this can be cleared up."

"I think Sofia has a point, Angelo," Miriam said.

Angelo shrugged. "Perhaps, you're right. I'll sleep on it." He looked at his watch. "It's getting late. If you don't mind, I'm going to turn in."

"Yes, I'm tired too." Sofia yawned. "You're sure you don't mind sleeping on the couch?"

"Certainly not," Angelo said.

Chapter 32

Sofia woke from a dream about Nicholas when she heard loud voices. The bedroom lamp on the nightstand was on and Miriam was sitting up in bed.

"What's wrong?" Sofia whispered.

"I don't know. I think it's two men and they're arguing with Angelo."

Sofia checked her watch. It was four o'clock in the morning. They both got up and dressed fast. Fortunately, they'd slept in their underwear and T-shirt. The voices got angrier and now Sofia understood part of the argument.

"*Dove sono le donne*?" one of the men yelled. "Where are the women?"

"*Sono ritornate*, they've gone back." She heard Angelo say. He talked loudly. Was he trying to warn Miriam and herself?

"We have to hide," Miriam hissed. She slid her backpack under the bed. Sofia did the same. They pulled the cover over the bed to make it look unused. They grabbed their shoes and checked quickly if anything personal was lying around. Miriam switched off the light, they stepped into the walk-in closet, and closed the door. Just in time.

The door to the bedroom opened with a bang and someone stepped inside. Sofia held her breath, her knees were shaking. She was sure they were able to hear her heart pound in her chest.

"*Andate*, gone," a male voice said. It sounded familiar to Sofia. The door slammed shut. Miriam carefully slid the closet door open, so they were able to hear better.

"I think it's the cop." Sofia's heart filled with dread. It was her fault. The guys had followed them all the way to Angelo's house. She had practically brought them here.

"You're dead." Someone shouted. "We have orders to eliminate you."

"Cricket? Or should I say, Anton Leonardi, the mobster?" Angelo said, his voice dripping with sarcasm.

"Shut up." There was a slapping sound.

Sofia felt a hand on her arm. "Do you know how to shoot a gun?" Miriam whispered.

"No." Then a memory rose in Sofia's mind. Henry, her father, had had a gun. He'd kept it locked up, but one time there had been a few burglaries in the neighborhood. So he'd taken it out, cleaned it, and showed Sofia how to use it. "Just in case," he'd said.

"Maybe," Sofia whispered.

"There may be a gun in the nightstand. Angelo always used to keep one next to his bed. Loaded." Miriam gave Sofia a probing look, as if to assess her courage.

Sofia tiptoed out of the closet, her knees wobbly, her heart pounding. What if they came into the room again? She held out her arms in the dark and found the edge of the bed. With one hand on the bed, she felt her way to the nightstand and switched the lamp back on. She pulled the drawer open, which made a squeaky sound. The weapon was inside. Sofia faltered, then picked up the gun, and rushed back into the closet, no longer trying to be quiet. Fortunately, the argument in the living room drowned out all the other noise.

Sofia examined the gun. It looked somewhat similar to the one her father had owned. Her hand was trembling, but she gripped the handle and curled her finger around the trigger. She glanced at Miriam. "Ready to shoot." Her attempt at humor didn't make her feel calmer. She took deep breaths.

In the meantime, Miriam had discovered a piece of metal rod in the closet. "We have to act fast. Here's what I think. I'll stand next to the door and bang against it. The guys will come in. I'll be hidden by the door and I'll hit the first one. You shoot the other one."

"I don't know if I can shoot anyone. What if I miss? What if I kill him? I don't know how many bullets are in the pistol? What if it's not loaded?"

"It *is* loaded. I'm sure. We have to do it. They'll kill Angelo." Miriam sounded desperate.

Sofia felt she was going to faint. But she couldn't let them kill her great-uncle. She'd come so far to find him. "Okay," she whispered, her voice shaking.

"Ready?" Miriam asked.

"Yes … but please be careful." Sofia grabbed her arm.

Miriam nodded but her face showed fear. She tiptoed to the door, positioned herself on the side the door would open to. She waited a few seconds. Sofia's heart went into overdrive again, out of fear for Miriam and for herself. Miriam banged the pipe against the door. The argument in the other room stopped. A brief exchange of words. Sofia lifted the gun and pointed it at the door. Her hand was shaking so hard, she was afraid she'd drop the weapon. *Dear God, please help.*

Then everything happened at once. The door flew open. A scraggly-looking short man stepped into the room, holding a gun. Miriam, standing behind him, lifted the rod and hit him over the head, yelling at the same time. The blow made him tumble forward, his knees buckled, and he dropped the gun. Immediately, the second guy—the police officer Sofia had met—rushed into the room. He looked down at his friend, then turned to face Miriam. He, too, had a gun. Sofia pulled the trigger. The policeman yelled, dropped the gun, sunk to the floor, and grabbed his leg. An acrid smell filled the room. Sofia, no longer able to stand, slid down, her back propped against the closet wall, the gun still clutched in her hand. Darkness threatened to overwhelm her.

"You can let go now." She heard the calm voice of Angelo. She opened her eyes. He gently prodded her fingers open, took the gun from her, and helped her stand up. Miriam, standing next to them, held the guns of the two men in her hand. Angelo took them both, put them into the closet, and closed the closet door. The man Miriam had struck down began to move. He moaned and held his head. The policeman, still holding his injured leg, yelled at them in Italian.

"Miriam, there is some rope in the kitchen cabinet next to the sink. Can you get it?" Angelo said.

"Okay, just a moment." Miriam left the room.

Sofia, having gotten up in the meantime, was holding on to the closet door. Her knees were still trembling.

Angelo held her by the arm. "Brave woman. Nicholas can be proud of you."

Sofia managed a quick chortle. "He'd kill me if he knew."

Miriam came back with the rope. Angelo checked his gun. "There are still plenty of bullets here." He glared at the two guys on the floor. He held the handle of the pistol out to Sofia. "Would you do me the honors? Just shoot them if they don't cooperate." Sofia looked at the weapon, then met his eyes. He winked at her. "Just don't shoot me."

Having recovered somewhat, Sofia took the gun and held it pointed at the two men. Whereas before, the feeling of the gun in her hand had terrified her, now it gave her a sense of power. She held the pistol firmly in her hand. She wondered if she could ever actually kill a person.

Angelo and Miriam proceeded to tie the hands of the two men behind their backs. The one guy who had been hit over the head was slowly recovering from the blow and began to squirm. Angelo held him by the arms while Miriam wrapped the rope around his wrists. "Stop fighting or you're going to have a bullet in your head." Angelo motioned with his head toward Sofia. "She won the NRA shooting competition for women last year."

Tying up the fully awake but injured cop was more difficult. "Are you crazy? I'm hurt. Are you going to tie up an injured man? I thought we were friends."

"All of a sudden we're friends again? Just a few minutes ago, you were going to kill me," Angelo said. He pulled the man's arms behind his back. Fabio screamed. "Hold still and it won't hurt as much."

After binding their hands, Angelo proceeded to tie their legs as well under the loud protests and filthy expletives of both men. He checked the wound on Fabio's leg. "Just a scratch. Don't whine like a baby."

"Are you going to let us die here?" Fabio's eyes registered fear.

"Don't worry. You deserve it, but we aren't killers. After we leave, I'll call the police and the ambulance to come and get you." Angelo double-checked the bindings and got up.

"Don't call the police, for God's sake," Fabio screamed, trying to wiggle his hands free.

"Why not? Are you afraid they'll find out about the illegal crap you've been involved in? That you were going to kill someone at the behest of a mobster in the United States?" Angelo smirked.

"Okay, ladies, let's go." Angelo grabbed a bag with some clothes and other essentials, his passport, and money. Sofia and Miriam pulled their backpacks from under the bed. On the way out, Angelo took a small chain with a round ornament from the wall and put it around his neck. "The medal of Saint Benedict," he said in answer to Sofia's questioning look. "For good luck."

Angelo locked the house but put the key under a flower pot next to the door. He walked around the house to his car. Miriam and Sofia followed.

Outside, it was getting light. The early morning mist hovered over the trees. Angelo turned around. "Thank you, you women are amazing. You saved my life." He hugged them both.

When they arrived at the car, Angelo dropped his bag on the ground. "Damn it all, the assholes slashed my tires."

Sofia scanned the area. "How did they get here? Where is their car?"

"Over there," Miriam pointed at a jeep parked behind a tree.

"Well, I've always wanted to drive a jeep," Angelo said. "Wait here." He walked back to the house, unlocked the door, and went inside. He came back a few minutes later, holding up a pair of car keys.

He opened the door of the jeep. Sofia motioned for Miriam to sit in the front seat but Miriam climbed into the back. When they were all seated, Angelo started the car.

"What did you mean when you said I won the NRA shooting competition?" Sofia asked him.

He looked at her. His face stretched into a full-blown smile. It was the first time she saw his smile reach his eyes. "Didn't you?" He gave her a mock-surprised look.

"I don't even know what it is," she said.

"Neither do I." He grinned.

Chapter 33

They drove slowly down the rugged road, trying to avoid the potholes. The jeep, however, was made for streets such as these and lumbered over the uneven spots without any problems.

Angelo was quiet, deep in thought. Images of the past night tumbled through his mind. They had barely survived a vicious attack. If he hadn't been for Miriam and Sofia, he might be dead. Of course, the women had brought the criminals to his door. Rather than being angry or regretting it, he felt a sense of relief. He knew now what he had to do. He was afraid of the consequences. Anton was still around. He was still a threat. And there was the murder of Fred. Angelo suspected that Anton was behind that as well. Who else could it be? But if the police in California suspected Angelo of killing Fred, he would probably be arrested and would spend time in jail. What if he couldn't prove his innocence? He just had to trust. He couldn't go on hiding any longer. But first he had to find a place to stay until he was ready to leave. Should he accept Sofia's invitation to go to Tuscany?

"Where are you going to go?" Sofia asked, as if she had picked up on his thoughts.

"I don't know." Angelo said.

"You can stay at my apartment," Miriam suggested.

Angelo shook his head. "Thanks, but I'm afraid they'd find me there. They must have followed you, which means they know where you live. In fact, you shouldn't go back home right away. I don't want anything to happen to you."

"I have a better idea," Sofia said. "As I told you, I have a place in Tuscany. Why don't you both come with me? There's enough room. Miriam you can stay as long as you want, until this thing is cleared up. And Angelo needs to return to California anyway. We can leave together from there."

Miriam shook her head. "I have to go to work tomorrow. I teach kindergarten."

"Couldn't someone fill in for you?" Angelo asked. He wanted Miriam to be with him. He felt bad for having abandoned her and wanted to have some time to try to make things right, to reconnect.

"No, not at such short notice. But I'll stay with my mother for a few days. She lives nearby, and I should be safe there." Miriam put her hand on Angelo's shoulder. "I promise I'll be careful. You need to go back and take care of things."

Sofia turned around. "We'll have to keep in touch."

"Yes," Miriam said. "Either here, or I'll visit you in California. I haven't been back to the States for a long time."

Angelo glanced at Miriam in the rearview mirror. "I'll be in touch, too. I promise." He hesitated. "That is if you want me to."

"Yes." Miriam squeezed his shoulder. "Not that you deserve it," she grumbled under her breath.

"Yes, I know." Angelo cleared his throat. "Okay, this is what we'll do. I'll drop the jeep off at the parking lot. They'll find it eventually. Then we'll take you guys' car and drive to Miriam's place to pick up Sofia's car. I also need to stop by the monastery and let Abbot Francesco know what happened and that I need to leave. Agreed?"

"Yes," Sofia said. "What about the guys in your house? One of them is hurt. Doesn't he need a doctor?"

"The bullet didn't penetrate. It's a superficial wound. Fortunately, I have a friend who may be able to help me out with that. I'll call him from the parking lot." He glanced at Sofia with a humorous glint in his eyes. "I think you shook a little too much when you pulled the trigger."

"Thank God," Sofia said. "I couldn't live with myself if I'd actually killed the man. Not even a criminal like him."

They arrived at the end of the bumpy mountain path and drove on the paved road into Rivalta to the parking lot. Angelo parked the car next to Miriam's.

Miriam checked the windshield. "We're lucky. No ticket."

"This is a public lot, so it's okay to leave it overnight," Angelo said. "And it's one of the few where you don't have to pay."

They grabbed their bags and backpacks and piled into Miriam's car. Angelo pulled out his cell phone. "Just a moment." He pressed a button.

"Pronto," said a groggy voice.

"Larry? It's … Danilo," Angelo said. He had almost used his real name, having gotten used to it again around Miriam and Sofia. "Did I wake you?"

"It's okay. I have to get up anyway. We had a little … well get-together with a few guys last night." The voice sounded clearer now.

"Drinking party, huh?" Angelo said.

"One of the perks of unemployment," Larry said, then gave a snort. "What can I do for you?"

"Remember Fabio?"

Silence. Then: "Are you trying to ruin my day?"

"No, not at all. I just found an opportunity for you to get back at him. This time for sure."

Another moment of silence. "This better be good."

Angelo briefly related the events of the past night. "Fabio was asked to eliminate me. Fortunately, I have two brave friends with me." He glanced at Miriam and Sofia. "We managed to tie them up and leave them in my house. Fabio is a little hurt, nothing serious."

"Who wants to eliminate you?" Larry asked.

"It's a long story and has to do with things that happened back in California. I'll tell you another time. Right now, I need for someone to pick the two guys up at my cabin. Key is under the flower pot next to the door. Fabio may need a doctor. Can you arrange this?"

"May I kill him instead?" Larry asked.

"It's up to you, but I have a better idea. I have real evidence that Fabio is involved in illegal dealings, exporting stolen art works from Italy to the United States. He delivers them to a man who is involved with the mob and has killed someone, actually I think two people, probably more. He ordered Fabio to kill me, because I know too much about him. I know it sounds crazy, but you have to trust me for the moment. I'm on my way to write this all down and I will testify if I need to. This could be the greatest story of your life. You will be back in demand again."

He heard a sigh at the other end. "Danilo, this is about the most outrageous and craziest story I've heard in a long time. And I'm supposed to believe it?"

"Larry, it's true. I'll tell you everything later."

Another sigh. "All right. I'll see what I can do. But you better give me all the details."

"Thanks, Larry, you won't regret it." Angelo pressed the disconnect button and nodded at Miriam. "Ready to go."

"What was that all about?" Sofia asked.

Chapter 34

"Larry is an investigative journalist, originally from England," Angelo explained as they were driving toward Moretta.

"We met years ago in Bardonico when he did a news report on the corruption and illegal activities of government officials. When Fabio threatened me and I left Bardonico, I contacted Larry. I suggested he look into the police department in Bardonico, that I had been approached by someone with an offer that sounded suspicious to me. I gave him as much information as I could without directly exposing Fabio. I still felt a certain loyalty to him, since we'd been friends. Also I didn't know if he actually went through with the deal of smuggling art works or if he took my advice.

"Anyway, Larry looked into the matter and accused him and the department in an article in the paper of corruption and illegal smuggling. The problem was he didn't have enough proof and the source he got some of the information from wasn't reliable. He got into a lot of trouble and was fired from his job."

"Were you the unreliable source?" Miriam asked.

"No, I wasn't. Well, indirectly I guess I was when I encouraged him to look into the department. In the meantime, I lost touch with Larry. I heard about the whole thing after the fact by accident. I felt I was in part responsible for Larry's downfall. I either should have given him the whole story and named Fabio, or I shouldn't have said anything at all. I tried to contact him. It took me a while, but I finally got a hold of him.

"We met and we talked. He didn't blame me. He understood that I didn't want to name a former friend. He said he'd done shoddy work in his eagerness to crack down on police corruption. Still I felt bad, that in a way I'd betrayed him. Had I known that Fabio would even consider killing me, I wouldn't have hesitated to expose him.

"In hindsight, I suspect that Fabio believed I had ratted on him and that this was the reason for the investigation of his department. That's why he tried to track me down and found out I was in Moretta."

"Oh, my God." Miriam exhaled deeply. "What an ordeal. I just wish you had confided in me."

Angelo lifted his hands with palms turned up. "Yes, I know, I should have … but, once again, I panicked."

"Perhaps now, after all this happened, your friend will be exonerated," Sofia turned around to face Angelo, who sat in the back seat.

"I hope so," he said. "I hope this whole thing comes out in the open and the people responsible will get punished."

Angelo looked pensive and the lines in his face seemed to have deepened over the past few hours. Sofia knew he was worried. He'd been hiding for twenty years. Coming out of hiding and facing his family and possible murder charges must be terrifying.

"If for some reason we should be questioned about the incident up in my house," he continued, "I think we should say that I shot Fabio."

"Why?" Sofia asked.

"I have a permit for the weapon. I speak the language, and I wouldn't want you to get into trouble."

"But it was self-defense," Miriam said. She started the car and drove it out of the parking lot and onto the street toward Moretta.

"Yes, but the jerks may deny it. There might be an investigation. Sofia could be arrested, questioned. She'd need a lawyer, and it could be very unpleasant, to say the least. I don't want you to be involved any more than you already are."

Sofia's heartbeat increased. She hadn't even thought about the possible consequences. "But you'd be in trouble, too," she said.

Angelo gave a quick laugh. "I'm already in trouble up to my ears, Sofia. One problem more or less won't make any difference."

"But what if he says I shot him. He saw me, didn't he?" Sofia said.

"I don't think he was aware of it. It happened too fast. Besides, he'd be all too happy to put the blame on me. He's too macho to admit that a woman got the better of him. So, let's agree, I shot him, okay?"

Sofia felt his sharp eyes watching her. She turned around. "Okay."

They lapsed into silence. Sofia, her thoughts racing, tried to calm down and enjoy the sun-dappled hills and the vineyards outside. It didn't work. For the first time since she began her search for the mysterious and missing great-uncle, she felt she was way over her head in this adventure. Investigation, possible jail, what would her family, Nicholas, say? She'd found Angelo but perhaps lost her freedom in the process.

"Do you really think I could get arrested?" Her voice trembled.

She felt a strong hand on her shoulder. "No. I don't think so. I just want to cover all the bases." Angelo's voice sounded reassuring again.

In the meantime, they had arrived at Miriam's house in Moretta. They went inside and Angelo walked through all the rooms, then came back into the living room.

"Just wanted to make sure everything is okay," he said, meeting Miriam's puzzled look.

"Why would they bother with me?" Miriam asked.

Angelo shrugged. "As long as we don't know who's behind Fabio, we better be very careful. There are people out there for whom human life means nothing. Believe me. So I really want you to pack some things and spend a few nights at your mother's. We can drive you there."

"I can drive there myself. It's actually within walking distance. I need to take care of some stuff first, water the plants and the yard. They wouldn't be coming for me today. They're probably still tied up in your house." Miriam opened the refrigerator. "Would you like some lunch or coffee or something."

Angelo glanced at his watch. "We better get going. I still need to drive by the monastery to talk to Abbot Francesco. I hope you don't mind?" He turned to Sofia.

"No problem," she said.

"Well, then, but please Miriam go to your mother today, okay? And call me when you get there. Do you have my cell phone number?" Angelo's dark eyes darted around the room as if he wanted to make sure nobody was hiding in a corner somewhere.

Sofia, wanting to give them some privacy, picked up her bag. "I'll get my car out of the garage."

"Okay," Miriam said. "The door is unlocked."

Sofia and Miriam hugged. "Please stay in touch," Miriam said. "Let me know how everything turns out."

Sofia nodded. "Yes, of course. I'll see you again, either here or in California. Thank you very much for your help. I dragged you into a dangerous situation. I'm sorry."

"It was exciting. Getting to know you and finding this faithless friend here again was worth it." Miriam gave Angelo a pointed look.

Sofia opened the front door and glanced left and right before she stepped outside. No blue Honda. She shook her head, realizing that whoever drove that car must have been one of the guys now sitting tied up in Angelo's house. Waiting for Angelo after backing her car out of the garage, she wondered if she would ever forget those dangerous moments in Angelo's house. Her heart still constricted at the thought of having shot someone. She could've killed the man. She couldn't even remember if she had aimed at a particular part of his body. The moment before she pulled the trigger was a blur. The only thing stuck in her mind was the pressure of her finger pulling the trigger, the crack of the gunshot, and the smell of something burning.

A light tap at the passenger window brought her back to reality. Sofia unlocked the door. Locking it while she was waiting must be another unconscious reaction to the turbulence of the past days.

Angelo put his bag on the backseat and got in. "You're sure you don't mind driving by the monastery?"

"No," Sofia said. "I think the abbot will be relieved when he sees you. I hope we didn't tell him anything you didn't want him to know. At least he didn't act surprised, and he said you should go back and take care of things."

"Yes, he knows me quite well," Angelo said softly.

They were quiet on the short stretch toward the abbey. At one point, a blue Honda drove from a side street into main road and Sofia flinched.

"What's the matter?" Angelo asked.

Sofia shook her head. "Nothing. I just get scared every time I see a blue car.

At the monastery, they got out and walked into the courtyard. Angelo pointed at the stone bench along the wall of the chapel. "Wait here, I'll go find Abbot Francesco."

Sofia sat down and waited. The sun was gaining strength, and it promised to be a warm day. Next to the chapel was a blooming tree with purple blossoms. She closed her eyes and tried to relax, inhaling the sweet-pungent scent of some kind of herb. Hearing footsteps, she opened her eyes again. A few monks in black walked by, glanced at her, and nodded, giving her a silent greeting. Shortly thereafter, Angelo came back out followed by the abbot, who greeted her with a smile. "You found each other. Wonderful."

Sofia got up and shook hands with him. "Yes, thank God."

"Thank God, indeed," he replied. He turned to Angelo. "I'll explain your absence to the youngsters. They will understand and Agosto will be a good substitute." Angelo and the abbot hugged. "Go with God," Abbot Francesco said. "I'll see you when you get back. All will be well."

PART FIVE: THE JOURNEY HOME

Chapter 35

It was quiet in the car. Angelo took deep breaths, trying to get his emotions under control. Saying goodbye to the abbot, the man who had helped him through difficult times since he met him four years ago, was tough. So was leaving Miriam so soon after meeting her again. Being near her had revived those feelings he'd tried hard to deny for so long. He hoped they could stay in touch.

However, it had been Abbot Francesco, with his compassion and tolerance, who had helped Angelo to truly turn his life around. They'd met at a time Angelo was rudderless and lost. He wanted to join the monastery, longing for peace and stability. He was tired of hiding and fleeing. The abbot, however, saw right through him. He knew that his wish to become a monk was just another escape.

"Do you really think that you can run away from your life and hide behind the walls of the abbey?" he had said. "That's not how it works. Don't you realize you're taking yourself and your problems with you? You're just relocating them. You have to deal with yourself and your issues in the outside world. You can come here to pray and to ask God for guidance. But you have to live in the world."

The abbot had helped him find work as an administrator in a school in Rivalta and encouraged him to work with troubled youth. "You of all people know what it means to be lost. You may be able to help them. But in order to do this, you have to help yourself. You have to forgive yourself. And ask God for forgiveness. Show the boys through your example that there is always hope and the Lord will never forsake them."

And Angelo had done it. For the first time in his life, he had felt that he was doing something worthwhile. He felt needed, he had a task to fulfill. It wasn't easy. Some of the boys warmed up to him quickly. He never preached to them. He just told them how badly he had messed up. They could relate to his stories. However, some of the hard-core youngsters were too far gone for him to help them. He had to learn that it really wasn't up to him. It was up to destiny. To God? He still had doubts about the existence of the god that Don Ambrosio, Abbot Francesco, and the monks believed in. But each small achievement in his work with the boys, each genuine smile on their faces gave him the feeling that there was a benign force at work that went beyond his feeble strength.

And now? What would happen? Would he be able to return to his work with them? He already missed them: Mario, with his gap tooth, Enrico covered by tattoos, Giorgio, the star of the soccer team.

And then there was Sandro. He had grown to love him and they had become very close. Would the boy feel abandoned again? What would happen to him now? Abbot Francesco had promised to take care of him as well as he could. Angelo just had to trust.

His interest in religion and a religious life had begun with Don Ambrosio, the gentle priest, who had accepted him the way he was. He had been available when he needed to talk but had never pried. He had been a true Christian, accepting, forgiving, honest but never preachy.

"Do you want to stop in Bardonico to talk to Don Ambrosio?" Sofia asked.

Angelo gave her a puzzled look. How had she guessed who he was thinking about? "Thanks, but it would be too far out of the way. It's north and we're going south, aren't we?"

"We have to drive north first. I have to return some things to my friend in Pavone. So it wouldn't be too much out of the way."

"It's Fabio's territory though," Angelo said after a pause. "I may not want to show my face there until I know what's going to happen to him. The police department is right across the *piazza* from the church. We may get arrested."

"Can't you call your journalist friend and find out?"

"I can try." Angelo pulled his cell phone out of his pocket, then turned to Sofia. "Are you hungry?"

"A little."

"Let's stop somewhere for a bite to eat," Angelo suggested.

They were on the freeway north toward Pavone. Sofia exited at the next rest stop. They got out of the car and stretched. Angelo tried to call Larry to ask him about the situation with Fabio and his cohort. However, he just got the answering machine and left a message. They went inside and bought sandwiches, juice, and coffee and sat down at one of the tables.

"Not exactly the fanciest of foods," Angelo said. "But it's at least a snack."

"It's okay. I really don't think I ever had bad food in Italy," Sofia said.

Angelo agreed. "That's one thing they're really good at. Well, one of many things." He glanced at his watch. "We probably shouldn't stay here too long. Once rush hour starts, the freeways can be a bitch."

Sofia grinned. "Should you be cursing as a Benedictine monk?"

"Well, I'm not a real monk, I'm an oblate, but you're right, I shouldn't be cursing." Angelo gave a quick chortle and pulled on his short beard.

"Do you want to be a full monk, or whatever that's called?" Sofia asked.

"That's a really big commitment. It would mean a life of work, prayer, and celibacy. I know that Abbot Francesco wants me to be a lay monk and live outside the monastery. Oblates can be in a relationship or marry. He's probably right," Angelo said.

"Are you thinking of getting married again sometime in the future?" Sofia took a sip of water. She watched Angelo over the rim of her glass.

"I haven't had much luck with being married," he said, then lapsed into silence. Thoughts of Elvira flooded him. The scar of losing her and feeling responsible for her accident still throbbed in his heart.

"What about Miriam?" Sofia asked.

Angelo raised an eyebrow. "You ask difficult questions."

"I'm sorry. I don't mean to pry."

"It's okay." Angelo leaned back in his chair and glanced out the window. "I think once I'm out of the mess I'm in, I may see more clearly. Right now, I can't even begin to think about relationships or romance."

"I understand," Sofia said. They were quiet for a while. She drank the rest of her water and put down her glass. "Let's go."

They left the rest stop and drove north. Traffic was already getting heavy on the freeway and the toll stations where Sofia had to pay, since she didn't have a pass, slowed the trip even more. However, they got to Pavone in a little over two hours.

In Pavone, Sofia's friend, Tina, welcomed them enthusiastically. She overwhelmed Angelo with a flood of words expressing her joy that the *"figliol prodigo,"* the prodigal son, or rather the *"prozio prodigo,"* the prodigal great-uncle, was found. *"Bravo, bravo,"* she said and patted Angelo's arm. She joked around and insisted that they have dinner with her before driving to Tuscany.

Angelo was taken by her friendliness. It had been a while since someone welcomed him with such fervor. The elderly woman, a little on the heavy side, with a kind wrinkled face reminded him of his mother and a feeling of nostalgia flooded him.

Sofia and Angelo wanted to take Tina out to dinner, but she wouldn't hear of it. She marched into the kitchen and whipped together a delicious spaghetti al pesto meal with a mixed salad. She offered them a glass of wine but Sofia and Angelo declined since they still had quite a long drive ahead of them. They finished their meal with the usual espresso and a slice of homemade lemon pie.

With a lot of best wishes, hugs and kisses, they left. Angelo suggested he drive part of the way, but Sofia's rental agreement was only for her as driver. Since they didn't want to get into trouble during a possible traffic control, Sofia said she didn't mind driving. It was a little after seven o'clock in the evening and the drive should take about four and a half hours. If traffic wasn't bad, they would reach Vignaverde close to midnight.

South of Genoa, traffic eased up a bit. What slowed them down, however, was increasingly bad weather in Tuscany. It started with a drizzle, which developed into a full rainstorm with flashes of lightening. Sofia had to stop a few times to avoid the flooded parts of the highway.

Angelo could feel Sofia's tension, and he himself kept a foot on an imaginary brake. Near Florence, the rain stopped and they both breathed a sigh of relief.

"Typical rainstorm in Tuscany," Sofia said. "It feels like pandemonium, and then it just stops and everything is calm again."

"Just like the people in Italy." Angelo snickered. "They blow up fast, throw up their hands, you think they're going to kill you. And the next moment, they smile again."

"Isn't that the truth?" Sofia said. "Well, we're getting close. We'll soon be in Vignaverde."

Angelo had been to Tuscany before but he had only visited Florence and Siena. He was looking forward to getting a glimpse of the smaller towns and the vineyards. "You've never told me how you got a hold of property in Tuscany," he said.

"It's a long story," Sofia remarked.

He smiled. "Well, we're used to long stories by now."

"That's true. I'll tell you all about it once we're there," Sofia said. "Look, that's Vignaverde itself. The estate is nearby."

Before them, up on the hill, Angelo saw the lights of the city, the lit up dome and the Etruscan walls. "Beautiful," he said.

After fifteen minutes, they drove up a small hill, at the bottom of which Angelo could make out a few buildings, storage or working sheds most likely. They parked the car next to two residential houses. It was dark, everybody seemed to be asleep. He glanced at his watch. It was after midnight. They got out of the car and Angelo tried to loosen his tight muscles from the long and at times intense drive.

They walked to the smaller of the two houses. Sofia turned on the outside lamp and dug into her purse, probably searching for the key. Angelo saw a few stone pines and what looked like a small olive grove next to the house. The house itself was built in the Tuscan style with the door topped by a stone arch.

"Home sweet home," Sofia said, as she pushed the door open. They stepped into a small hallway. Sofia stopped and stared at the wardrobe. "That's odd," she said.

"What's the matter?" Angelo asked.

"I don't remember having left these boots out here. What? ..." She shrugged, then opened the door to what looked like the living room. She snapped on the light and stopped again. "Shhh." She put a finger to her lips.

He could hear it too, now. Footsteps. Upstairs? He reached into his bag and pulled out the gun. "Stand behind me," he whispered and pulled Sofia back.

The footsteps were louder now. Someone was about to walk down the stairs. Angelo pointed the gun in that direction. He watched as the shadow of a person became visible at the top.

"Who's there?" a male voice called.

Chapter 36

"Nicholas?"

"Oh, it's you?" Nicholas was relieved when he heard Sofia's voice.

"My God, you scared me to death. What are you doing here?" Sofia asked, her pale face slowly gaining some color again.

Nicholas had taken a few steps down the stairs when he saw a man with a gun in his hand. He looked like Grandpa Martin, except for the short beard and the forbidding dark eyes that stopped Nicholas in his tracks. He raised his hands. "Don't shoot, please."

The man stared at him. "Nicholas? My God … you're a grown man."

Nonsensical as it seemed under the circumstances, this statement dissolved the tense situation.

"Uncle Angelo?" Nicholas slowly walked down a few steps.

Sofia hurried up the stairs and hugged him. She took his arm and walked him down the stairs. "I sure didn't expect you here? How? Why?"

"I was worried, for God's sake. I hadn't heard from you. I called the Santuccis and they hadn't heard anything either. The last you told me was that you were going to a monastery. I just got scared and so did Grandpa. I got here yesterday and I was going to drive to that friend of Edoardo's … Tina something."

"I tried to call several times from my cell, but it didn't work. And we were … well kind of busy." Sofia gave the man next to her a furtive glance.

Nicholas tried to wrap his mind around the fact that seemingly out of nowhere his long-lost great-uncle stood in front of him.

"Uncle Angelo?" he asked again, afraid that the figure in front of him might dissolve any moment.

The man cracked a quick smile. "Yes."

"Well, let's sit down somewhere," Sofia said. "My legs are still shaking from the shock. I sure didn't expect anybody in our house."

Nicholas's gaze fell again on the gun that was still in Angelo's hand. "You always carry a gun? Is that thing loaded?"

"Yes," his great-uncle said, as if carrying a gun was the most natural thing. Finally, he put the weapon back into his bag.

"You must live a dangerous life," Nicholas said.

"We had a few close encounters." Angelo spoke matter-of-factly.

"We?" Nicholas gave him a quizzical look. He noticed Sofia looking at his great-uncle imploringly.

"What's going on?" Nicholas said. "Are you guys okay?"

"I'll tell you all about it." Sofia brushed a strand of hair out of her face. "I need to sit down. We've been driving all the way from the Piedmont.

"Want something to eat?" Nicholas asked. "Or to drink? Wine? Coffee?"

"We had dinner in Pavone," Sofia said. "Maybe some tea. Ginger or chamomile?" she asked Angelo.

"I've never had ginger tea. I'll try it."

"Sit down and relax," Nicholas said. "I'll make the tea." He walked into the kitchen and put the kettle on the stove.

Back in the living room, Sofia sat on the sofa, her legs stretched out. Angelo sat in an easy chair. Only now did Nicholas see how tired they looked.

"You're beat. How long have you been driving? Where are you coming from?" He sat down next to Sofia and put his arm around her, then shook his head as he looked his great-uncle up and down. "My God, I still can't believe you're here. We've been looking for you." He glanced at Sofia. "Did you tell him … about the bones and all?"

"Oh, yes. I told him everything."

The kettle whistled. Nicholas went back into the kitchen and poured the boiling water over the tea bags. He brought the cups and some cream and sugar and set them on the coffee table. Sofia handed Angelo a cup and took one herself.

Nicholas stared at Angelo transfixed. "Do you realize you may be a suspect?"

Angelo shrugged. "Doesn't surprise me. I didn't do it though. But I think I know who did. Or at least who ordered it done."

"Well they need you to testify. Why didn't you contact us for such a long time?" Nicholas asked.

"There are many reasons. It's a long story." Angelo sighed. "I guess I've said that many times. I'm a little too tired tonight to tell you everything. But just for now, Fred was my friend. He and I did some work for his cousin Anton Leonardi. During one of the jobs, we witnessed Anton kill someone in cold blood. He saw us. We knew we were dead if he caught us. We decided to disappear separately. I went to our relatives in New York … you know about that."

Nicholas nodded. "Yes."

"Then, as you know, I left for Italy. I've been hiding there and tried to start a new life, away from all the mess I was in back home. But I'm tired of running. I need to go back and at least try to clear my name. I feel terrible about Fred's murder."

"When did you leave for New York and for Italy?" Nicholas asked.

Angelo scratched his head. "I left for New York on July 27. I still remember the day. It was my mother's birthday. The year was 1992. I stayed in New York for two weeks and then left for Italy."

"Then, if Fred was killed later, you would have an alibi," Nicholas said. "And the relatives in New York can verify when you got there and when you left."

"I don't know if they can pinpoint the day of his murder that well from a skeleton after such a long time." Angelo suppressed a yawn.

"Well, I'm sorry to keep you up. You're tired. Let's talk tomorrow." Nicholas got up. "We should call Grandpa, though. You want to talk to him?"

Angelo shook his head. "Not tonight ... well, not today ... or rather I'll talk to him *later* today." He glanced at his watch. "I couldn't possibly deal with something that emotional without some sleep first."

"I understand," Nicholas said.

"I'll show you your room." Sofia got up.

Chapter 37

Anton Leonardi stood by the window, gazing at the fog on Lake Michigan.

It was the end, he knew it. The jerk who had killed Fred and was to take care of Angelo had disappeared. Of course, the ass didn't know who gave the order to assassinate Fred and Angelo. Louie was trying to find him but so far without success. If Louie got caught, he would sing. Why wouldn't he? He would look out for number one, couldn't even blame him. Information in exchange for a lighter sentence. Plea bargain.

And Louie had another important piece of information. He knew that Anton had killed Eppolito. This by itself wouldn't be the worst. Anton narrowed his eyes. He still had a couple of close friends who would back up his story, his alibi, that he wasn't in California at the time. He would be arrested, but he still had a chance that they'd let him go. But at this point, not even a short stay in prison was an option for him.

Not after the news he had just received. Pancreatic cancer. The death sentence. His own personal capital punishment.

How did it come to this? Anton glanced outside again. The fog had lifted over the lake and the Chicago sun shone faintly through the smog.

"You're a complete failure," his father had said. "A disgrace to the family." Anton was fifteen, had done some stupid stuff, stolen some things and sold them, making a profit. Got caught. First-time offender, so he got away with a warning. But his father's words followed him. He wanted to please his dad, but no matter how hard he tried, nothing seemed to impress the old fart. It got worse when his mother died. She'd been the buffer between him and his father, had stood up for him. When she was gone, his dad lost all interest in his son.

Anton tried hard to become successful, and he succeeded. Started his own trucking business together with a friend. The money he made, however, wasn't enough. And then his lucky draw. Someone approached him with a smuggling deal. Drugs and art objects, in part from Italy. The money was great. He hesitated but not for long. And the first deal went through smoothly. It was the beginning of Anton's criminal life. He began to build connections with criminal organizations. It all went perfect; well, there were some slight mishaps. He did some time. But all in all, a perfect life. Dangerous, yes, but worth it.

Until the day, that stupid idiot, Eppolito, interfered and began to blackmail him, obviously a newbie to the 'Ndrangheta clan. Anton agreed to pay. He suggested a secret location. Either Eppolito was a bloody beginner in the mob, or he greatly underestimated Anton. You don't meet at a secret location to hand over blackmail money. You do it in a public place. Instead of the money, Anton brought his Beretta to the meeting and shot the idiot. He deserved it. And then those two guys showed up. They weren't supposed to be there to begin with. They had gone to the wrong place to deliver the goods. Stupid no-good losers.

Of course, they had to disappear. So Anton did the only thing he could do. Rather than incriminate himself even more, he ordered his closest and most loyal friend to take care of business. Hire someone to kill the two idiots and bury their bodies on the family property. At the time, Anton expected to inherit the Leonardi estate. He was the oldest son.

It was a shock when Anton realized that his father had changed the will and bequeathed the family property to his cousin. He could just hope that he wouldn't dig up the field and find the bodies. But years went by and Anton felt safe again. Until Frank, the goddamn loser, sold that field. Without consulting him. And Frank had promised to share the inheritance with Anton. "We're family," he had said. Yeah, right. Traitor.

And Louie had failed him too. Hired the wrong guy to take care of business. Stupid son of a bitch. Well, there was one more thing Anton needed to do. He was not about to end up in jail. They wouldn't get him that easily. He still had a few trump cards in his deck, well at least one.

Anton walked over to his desk, opened a drawer, and pulled out his gun, the shiny Beretta, a gift from a friend, dead now. Anton smirked. He played with the gun, twirled it, then put it down.

Suddenly, he bent over and groaned with pain, holding his stomach. "Damn it." He took deep breaths and slowly stood up straight. Sweat poured down his face, dripping into his beard. He wiped it away, then picked up the gun again.

There was a knock at the door. "Anton, lunch is ready," his wife called. A wife he'd been married to for fifteen years. He'd loved her once. But that was gone, too.

He caressed the gun. It felt good in his hand, a perfect fit.

Chapter 38

"How did you find Angelo?" Nicholas asked as he and Sofia got ready for bed. "The last time we talked on the phone you said you were going to the monastery."

"Yes, that's when we found out that the abbot of the Novalesa Abbey knew Angelo. Remember I told you that Don Ambrosio mentioned his interest in the religious life?"

Nicholas chuckled. "Oh, yes, I thought it was the most outlandish statement. My great-uncle, the criminal, wants to find God. I guess it was true after all."

"Anyway, the abbot told us that Angelo worked for a school in Rivalta as some kind of administrator. But he also worked with troubled youngsters through a program led by the monastery," Sofia said.

"Incredible." Nicholas shook his head. "Well, he has a lot of personal experience in that department."

Sofia told him that the abbot didn't give them Angelo's address because of privacy issues. But Miriam suggested they check out Rivalta where they used to hike. There was a cottage there that Angelo loved. She thought he might be there.

Sofia told him about their outing and about what happened during the night they spent at Angelo's.

When she started talking about the two criminals, she watched as Nicholas's eyes narrowed and his jaw clenched. She toned down the story somewhat and left out the fact that she shot the policeman, but she'd already said too much.

"Are you out of your mind?" Nicholas jumped off the bed he was sitting on while Sofia undressed. "I can't believe you … and that woman. Why didn't you wait until Angelo contacted you, as the abbot said?"

"Well, I was afraid that perhaps Angelo wouldn't contact me. We were so close to finding him, and then Miriam suggested the outing. It sounded innocent. And when we found Angelo, I knew he wasn't a killer. We had a long talk. He left because he was afraid, not because he killed someone. He wanted to protect—"

"That's not the point," Nicholas said, angry now. "You didn't even know that before you found him. We don't even know now for sure. We only have his word. He could be lying. You went ahead and put yourself in grave danger. Did you even think about me? What if you'd been killed?" He rubbed his head furiously.

Sofia had never seen him this angry. They'd had an occasional argument but nothing really serious. But now, he was livid. Sofia understood that he was worried, but it was over, she was safe. He hadn't even acknowledged the fact that she had found their great-uncle.

"Don't be so angry," she said. "Aren't you at least happy that Angelo is here?"

Nicholas glowered at her. "And you knew he had changed his name and didn't even feel the need to tell me? Or the police? You withheld important information that could've helped us find him. Instead you went to track him down alone. As if you were some kind of private investigator."

"I only found out about the name change from Don Ambrosio. I tried to tell you several times, but I couldn't get through on my cell, and—"

"Don't lie to me. You could've told me several times. You could've sent me a text. Why didn't you?"

"Okay, I hesitated because … I wanted to find him before the police did." Sofia thought it best to be honest. "I didn't tell you because I didn't want to cause you a dilemma."

"What dilemma?"

"Shhh. Don't be so loud. Angelo can hear us."

"I don't care. He's responsible for this whole mess."

"Nicholas, please, now you're being unfair."

Nicholas walked to the window and stared outside. Sofia followed him and put her hand on his back. She felt him stiffen. Why was he so angry?

"Nicholas, I held back because I didn't want the police to know until I myself knew a little more. I would've told you, but I didn't want to ask you to keep it a secret. I'm sorry. I know now this was wrong. But please try to understand. I was so caught up in the whole thing. I got all this information and I felt compelled to follow through.

"Look, I know this is a difficult situation. Grandpa has very mixed feelings about Uncle Angelo. But he also misses him very much. He's his brother after all. And I also know from experience what it means to have a broken family. I just wanted—"

"Well has it ever occurred to you that Angelo is my great-uncle, too? I would've loved to know about your progress. In fact he is *my* great-uncle more than he is yours." Now, he sounded whiny.

Sofia glared at him. "What do you mean, he's more your great-uncle than he's mine?"

"Well, you know what I mean. He's your great-uncle through marriage, but—"

"Oh, I see. He isn't really my great-uncle. I'm just an outsider, your family isn't really my family?" Sofia felt bursts of anger rise in her. "You know who you remind me of? You talk just like my ex-husband did."

"That's not true. How can you—"

"I don't want to argue any longer. I'm going to sleep." Sofia pulled the comforter back on the bed and lay down, her back turned to Nicholas's side of the bed. Now, she was angry as well. She could understand him being upset because he was worried about her, because he felt she had been careless. But Nicholas was jealous of her because she succeeded in finding *his* great-uncle. How childish was that?

They were lying next to each other in icy silence. Sofia felt tears prick her eyes. She had accepted Nicholas's family as her own and his words stung her. They reminded her of James, her former husband, to whom she had been married for two short but painful years. He, too, had made her feel like an outsider in his family. Too exhausted from the long day to drown in sadness, she fell asleep.

Chapter 39

A sun ray landing on Sofia's face woke her. She glanced at the clock; it was close to nine. The empty bed next to her told her that Nicholas was already up. She sighed, remembering their argument of the past night. His jealous outburst still rankled her. It was the first time they had gone to bed and fallen asleep with resentment lingering between them.

The bedroom door opened and the scent of espresso filled the room. "Good morning. There's fresh coffee downstairs. We're low on groceries. I'm going to town to get some stuff for breakfast." Nicholas, fully dressed, a guilty expression on his face, gave her a cautious look.

"Want me to come with you?" she asked.

"Not necessary. Angelo is up as well. Perhaps you can introduce him to the family. I saw Julietta outside," Nicholas said.

Sofia got up and followed him into the hallway. At the top of the stairs, Nicholas turned around. "I'm sorry about last night. I was just really worried. And I didn't mean to claim Angelo for myself. I guess I was a little jealous that you found him and had all those crazy adventures while I sat at home. I know it's stupid." He gave a sheepish grin. "I'm sorry." He took her hand.

He looked embarrassed and contrite and Sofia's anger vanished. "Believe me, I wish you'd been with me. Next time, we'll track down missing relatives together." She smiled.

"Next time? There better not be a next time," Nicholas grumbled and hugged her.

Sofia went into the bathroom and took a quick shower, then pulled on a pair of light pants and a T-shirt. She had noticed the night before that it was markedly warmer in Tuscany than in the Piedmont.

Downstairs, Angelo stood by the open patio door, talking on his cell phone. He gave her a quick smile and nodded a greeting. Sofia went into the kitchen and poured herself a cup of coffee. She came back in and pointed at her phone. "You can use our landline. It's cheaper."

"Thanks. I have unlimited calls within Italy." Angelo picked up his cup of coffee and took a sip.

"Did you sleep well?" Sofia asked.

"Yes, very well. I was totally beat and I wasn't even the one driving."

Sofia sipped her coffee, then cleared her throat. "Did you hear our argument?"

A flicker of amusement flashed across his face. "I heard raised voices but didn't know what it was about."

"Well, I told Nicholas how I found you and about the night at your place. He got really upset that I was snooping and didn't tell him everything. He was worried, of course. And then he said that you were after all *his* great-uncle and what was I doing chasing after you?" Thinking about the argument made her angry again.

To her surprise Angelo laughed. It was the first time she'd heard him laugh out loud. He caught himself. "I'm sorry. I didn't mean to make light of your disagreement with Nicholas. It just seems funny to me that anybody would be so eager to claim me as his or her relative. I'm not exactly the favorite member of the Segantino family."

"Now you know, we really do care about you. And whether Nicholas likes it or not, I do consider you my great-uncle as well."

"Thank you." Angelo smiled. "And I'm delighted to have you as my great-niece." Then in a more serious tone. "Nicholas is right. You did put yourself in danger by searching for me. But I can't really blame you. You did save my life. You and Miriam. I'm still amazed how level-headed and brave you two were when you heard those two crooks in my home."

"Well, after all, we did bring them to you," Sofia said. "Of course, we didn't mean to."

They sat quietly for a while, sipping coffee and glancing at the landscape. The sun lit up the flowers in the garden and the field of poppies nearby. There was a knock at the door and Sofia got up to open.

Julietta stood outside. "You're back? I saw your car. Nicholas got here the day before yesterday," she said, all excited. Sofia and Julietta hugged.

"Oh, my God," Julietta called out when she came inside. "Is this *zio* Angelo?"

Angelo gave her an amused look, "*Si*, I'm afraid so."

"This is fantastic." Julietta hugged him. "*Benvenuto*." She turned to Sofia. "Where did you find him? You have to tell me all about it. I have to let *Mamma* know."

"Okay," Sofia said. "Nicholas will be here right away and then we'll come over to say hello." She didn't want to exclude him and get him upset again about her monopolizing *his* great-uncle.

Julietta left and a few minutes later, Nicholas showed up with a bag of groceries. He carried it into the kitchen and unpacked some salami, rolls, eggs, and fruit.

"Were you able to get a hold of Grandpa?" Nicholas asked Angelo.

Angelo shook his head. "Haven't tried yet. But I did get a hold of Larry," he said to Sofia. "Fabio was arrested. I guess they had some other stuff on him, aside from the fact that he tried to kill me."

Nicholas stared at Angelo. "Who is Larry … and Fabio?"

Oh, no. He feels left out again. "Fabio is one of the gangsters I told you about yesterday," Sofia explained. "Larry got into trouble because of him. Well, you better tell him." She motioned with her head in Angelo's direction.

Angelo gave Nicholas a brief summary of the role Larry played in their adventure. Nicholas seemed satisfied. "But what about Grandpa? He needs to know you're here."

Angelo exhaled deeply. "I know. I'm a coward. I'm simply afraid to talk to him after twenty years. I know I have to do it and I want to."

"It'll be fine," Nicholas said. "He'll be so happy to hear that you're okay. Whatever happened twenty years ago, he loves you."

"Why don't *you* call him first, Nicholas?" Sofia suggested. "You can prepare him and it wouldn't be such a shock. What do you think?"

"Maybe you're right. Let's get it over with." Nicholas picked up the phone and gave Angelo a questioning look.

Angelo nodded. Nicholas dialed and glanced at his watch. "He must be home by now. I hope he's not in bed yet." After a few seconds: "Well, hello there, Grandpa. How are you? I got some news for you." He grinned at Angelo. "Are you sitting down? Good, okay. You want to talk to your long-lost brother?"

Sofia saw Angelo's face pale. He got up. His body looked stiff and his hand trembled lightly as he took the receiver.

"Let's give him some privacy," Sofia whispered.

They went outside and sat down on the chairs on the patio.

Chapter 40

Angelo swallowed. "Hello Martin." There was a lengthy silence. *Did he hang up?* "Martin?"

"My God, Angelo, I never thought I'd hear from you again." Martin's dark voice was thick with emotion. "How are you?"

"I'm fine, thanks. I'm sorry about not contacting you before. I ..."

"It's okay. But you need to come back. Did Nicholas tell you about Fred?"

"Yes, well actually Sofia did. She was the one who tracked me down. I didn't kill Fred. You have to believe me. I've done a lot of crappy things, but I'm not a murderer."

"I know that." Angelo heard Martin's somewhat muffled voice call Maria. "Still, you have to come back. They'll know it wasn't you."

"I hope so, Martin." He hesitated. "How has life been treating you?"

"Okay, Angelo. Everybody is fine. We have a few new people in the family. One of them you've met by now."

"Yes, Sofia is a wonderful person," Angelo said. "Nicholas is a very lucky man. I can't believe how grown-up he is. I missed so much being away."

"Yes, I know. We missed you, too. How have you been?"

"I've been fine, well for the most part. At least I've tried to stay out of trouble, and I have actually done some worthwhile work for a change."

"Nicholas mentioned something about a monastery, that you joined a monastery or tried to?"

"Not quite. I work for a Benedictine abbey, but as a lay person."

"Amazing." Martin sounded puzzled.

"I can imagine what you think," Angelo said. "This must be some kind of joke. It's true, though. But I'll explain once I see you. I have a lot of explaining to do."

"When are you coming back?" Martin asked.

"Nicholas and Sofia are making reservations," Angelo said. "As soon as they are finalized, we'll let you know."

"We heard that you renewed your American passport, so you should be able to travel without problems. The strange thing is, the police couldn't find any additional information about your whereabouts."

Angelo hesitated. "This is because I changed my name in Italy."

"Oh, I see. Well, that explains it. But … how was Sofia able to find you then?"

Angelo cleared his throat. "She'll have to explain that herself."

"Okay. Anyway, Angelo, we can hardly wait to see you again. I don't even know what you look like anymore."

"The same, only twenty years older." Angelo said. "I look forward to seeing you, too."

"Wait, Maria wants to say hello," Martin hurried to say.

Angelo felt his eyes tear up as he heard Maria's voice. "Hello, Angelo, it's so good hearing from you again."

"Thanks, Maria, you still sound the same. I bet you haven't aged at all."

"Oh, yes, I have." Maria chortled. "We've all aged, but the most important thing is, we're still here, right?"

"Right." Angelo tried to swallow the knot in his throat.

"Well, dear brother-in-law, Martin is overjoyed about the good news. We all are. We didn't know if we'd ever find you. But it sounds like we have a private detective in the family."

"Yes, you can say that."

"Come back soon, Angelo."

"I will, Maria. Real soon."

Angelo put the phone down and wiped his eyes. He took deep breaths and once he felt calmer again, he stepped outside on the patio. Nicholas and Sofia were sitting on the garden chairs.

"Everything okay?" Nicholas asked.

Angelo nodded.

"Ready to meet the family? Sofia's family?"

"Let's do it." Angelo forced a smile.

At the main house, the clatter of dishes from the kitchen told them that lunch was being prepared. Julietta, the girl he'd just met, was setting the table in the dining area of the living room.

"*Mamma*," Julietta called. "They are here."

A middle-aged woman, who looked like she could be Julietta's mother, came out of the kitchen to welcome them. She had the same chestnut-colored longish hair. Hers was streaked with gray and her eyes were dark whereas Julietta's eyes were that interesting kind of purplish-blue like Sofia's. The woman shook her finger at Sofia. "You scared us. When we didn't hear from you for a few days, we thought something happened to you."

"I know. I'm so sorry. The last few days were just too hectic for phone calls," Sofia said.

"I already gave her hell. But she did track down our great-uncle. May I introduce Angelo, the famous and infamous member of the Segantino family," Nicholas said with a flourish.

"More infamous than famous," Angelo said quietly. "I'm very pleased to meet you."

"This is wonderful," the woman said. "*Benvenuto.*" She shook hands with Angelo. "I'm Luisa, Julietta's mother and this is Donna, my mother. She pointed to an old woman who stepped into the room, carrying a large soup tureen filled with what looked like minestrone. She put it on the dining table and nodded at Angelo with a quick smile. "*Buongiorno.*"

"Oh, and here is my brother, Edoardo." Luisa motioned at the door, where a tall, slim man with dark hair and a short beard appeared. He gave a slight bow and shook hands with Angelo. "*Buongiorno, signore.*" His eyes were quizzical, but not hostile. Angelo recognized this look, this expression somewhere between suspicion and cautious acceptance. He had met with it often.

Angelo guessed that everybody in the family knew of his dubious reputation. The other members showed no hesitation and had greeted him warmly. This man, however, reserved judgment as to what he thought of this newcomer. Angelo appreciated his honesty.

They all sat down to lunch, which was plentiful and excellent. They started with the soup. Aside from *bistecca* or steak, there was an assortment of vegetables as well as risotto. Edoardo poured the wine, a Sangiovese.

Lunch was relaxing. They didn't ask Angelo any questions, for which he was grateful. In spite of a good night's sleep, he felt tired. His mind was still trying to digest all the changes over the past few days. He missed Rivalta already, his work with the school, the youngsters. He hoped that his assistant, a capable but still inexperienced young man, would be able to manage the job. He missed Abbot Francesco and, most of all, Miriam.

Seeing Miriam again had made him realize how much he still loved her. He had been wrong just disappearing, and he hoped they would meet again and she would eventually forgive him. He had been able to call Don Ambrosio from Vignaverde and explain the situation to him. All his friends had wished him well and had told him to come back soon.

Would he be able to? Would he be able to clear his name? Whenever he thought about what lay ahead for him in California, he felt his heart constrict. What if he couldn't prove his innocence and ended up in jail?

Somebody had asked him a question or said something to him. He realized that everybody was looking at him.

"I'm sorry, I was somewhere else with my thoughts," he apologized.

Edoardo smiled at him. "No problem. Luisa asked if you would like an espresso with dessert."

"Oh, thank you, yes, I'd love one," Angelo said to Luisa.

"Let's sit over there," Edoardo suggested and motioned at the sofa and easy chairs next to the glass door leading out to the patio. "Perhaps now, Angelo can tell us his story." He sounded determined and the message was clear. *I want to know if we are hosting a criminal."*

Chapter 41

Over coffee and ice cream, Angelo gave the family an overview of his life back in California, what made him leave and come to live in Italy, his work here, and, most of all, his sadness about the mistakes he'd made, his friend's death, and his fear of what awaited him back in California.

After he finished his story, Angelo looked drained. It was quiet in the room for a while. Abruptly, Edoardo got up and walked over to him. He put his hand on Angelo's shoulder.

"Thank you for sharing this with us. You have led an amazing life. Have faith. Things will turn out all right. God has forgiven you. Now, you must forgive yourself."

"*Grazie.*" Angelo took the last sip of his coffee, then got up. "I think I'm going to step outside, get some fresh air."

"Perhaps Nicholas and Sofia can show you the property?" Edoardo suggested.

"What do you think, Uncle Angelo?" Nicholas asked. "Unless you want to be by yourself."

"No, I'd love to see the estate. Thanks." Angelo seemed relieved.

The three of them went outside and took a leisurely walk past the houses toward the vineyards. On the way, Sofia told Angelo how she came to meet her sister and the Santucci family. She told him of the double life her father had lived, that he had hidden the fact that he'd had an affair with Luisa in Vignaverde, had fathered a child—her sister Julietta—and had bought two of the vineyards because the estate was in financial trouble and needed money. It was only after his death that Sofia found out about all of this.

After Sofia finished telling the story, Nicholas put his hand on Angelo's arm. "As you can see, Uncle Angelo, we are not the only family with an unsavory past."

Angelo gave a quick smile. "Indeed. But Sofia's story has a good outcome. She inherited two gorgeous fields of grapes." He pointed at the vineyards. "And a beautiful sister, and a family."

"Yours will have a good outcome, too, Uncle Angelo." Sofia gently touched his arm.

"I hope so. Whatever happens. It's better than hiding."

A little later, Julietta joined them. They walked past the vineyards, admired the Sangiovese and Merlot fields, the spring flowers in the meadows, and the stone pines and olive groves of the neighbors. The twittering of birds was drowned by the sound of the trimming machine, which drove between the rows of vines, cutting back the dense tops of the foliage.

At the bottom of the hill, Julietta opened the door to the underground cellar where all the wine barrels with the aging wine were stored in racks, four barrels high.

Memories flooded Sofia as she entered the cellar. She had almost been crushed by one of the huge barrels when she first came to Vignaverde. As they walked along the rows of barrels, she inhaled the slightly musty smell.

After climbing back up the steps of the cellar, Angelo stopped, his face pensive. He looked around the estate. "It all comes back," he said, quietly and put his hand on Nicholas's shoulder. "My brother's and your father's vineyards in California. I could've been part of it, had I not been the lazy and greedy bum I was."

"You can still be part of it, when you come back," Nicholas assured him. "We all need help, especially my father who runs like crazy all over the world taking part in contests and advertising rather than taking care of his vineyards."

"Then who does take care of them?" Angelo asked.

"My brother and sister and he has a slew of employees, but he's always short-handed."

"As much as I enjoyed my job at one of the vineyards in Italy," Angelo said, "I did it mainly to support myself. I don't have the passion for it. I guess this was one of the reasons, aside from my laziness, I never got into it back in California. My job as counselor, working with troubled youth is more meaningful to me."

"I know what you mean, Uncle Angelo … may I call you Uncle?" Julietta smiled at Angelo.

He put his hand briefly on her shoulder. "Of course, you may. You're my great-niece's sister, so yes, I'm your great-uncle, too."

"Well, I grew up on a vineyard," Julietta said. "I love to help out. I love our beautiful estate. But I decided not to become a vintner and winemaker like the rest of my family. I am more interested in science."

"Good for you," Angelo said. "You have to follow your heart when you choose something you're going to do the rest of your life. Or at least part of your life. Sofia told me you're going to study at Cal Poly in San Luis Obispo next spring."

Julietta nodded. "Yes, I am very excited about it … and very nervous."

Sofia hugged her. "No need to be nervous. You'll do well."

After their leisurely walk through the estate, Julietta returned to the main house and the others went back to Sofia's home. Angelo told them he'd like to take a brief nap.

He looked tired, the lines in his face seemed to have deepened.

"Angelo is worried about going back," Sofia said to Nicholas, as they sat on the patio, drinking lemonade.

"I'd be worried, too, if I were him. We don't really know what's going to happen," Nicholas said.

"You don't think, he's going to be arrested, do you?" Sofia asked.

Nicholas shrugged. "I have no idea. Grandpa didn't have any news when I talked to him last. From what I gather, they're still trying to figure out who killed Fred."

Chapter 42

Sofia, Nicholas, and Angelo spent a week in Vignaverde before their flight back to California. They took Angelo to the town of Vignaverde and showed him the neighborhood. It was a pleasant and, for the most part, relaxing time. Julietta accompanied them when she was free. She was a chatty young woman, who told him stories about her college and her life on the estate. She most of all helped Angelo take his mind off the upcoming return to the United States.

Although he was eager to see his brother and family again, he dreaded leaving Italy, his second or by now his first home, without knowing what would happen to him. Would he ever be able to return or would he end up in an American jail for a crime he didn't commit?

The few vacation days went fast and a week later, they said goodbye to the Santuccis and Sofia drove Angelo and Nicholas to the airport in Florence where she returned her rental car. They flew back via Frankfurt. On the plane, Angelo was able to sleep a little. As the plane descended toward the airport, his heart pounded.

In Los Angeles, they walked through customs without problems. When the customs officer asked Angelo how long he'd been abroad and he said twenty years, the man fixed him with a quizzical look. "You haven't been back for such a long time?"

Angelo shook his head. "No, this is my first time back. I probably won't recognize anything anymore."

The officer stared at the computer screen for quite some time and Angelo began to worry. Was there something about him being a fugitive? They might arrest him right there. "Well, welcome back," the man finally said and handed him back his passport.

"Thank you." Angelo took a relieved breath.

After the short flight to San Luis Obispo, they picked up their luggage and walked into the arrival lounge.

"Damn." Nicholas stopped.

"What's the matter?" Sofia asked, then exhaled deeply. "Bummer."

Angelo stared at them. "What?"

"It's the investigator I told you about, George Silver." Nicholas motioned with a quick movement of the head toward the exit.

"This is it," Angelo said with a sinking heart, as he examined the middle-aged, robust man with a crew cut walking toward them.

He nodded a greeting to Nicholas and Sofia, then faced Angelo with his sharp gray eyes.

"Angelo Segantino?" The voice wasn't threatening or unfriendly.

"Yes." Angelo's voice was trembling a little.

"It's been a long time," the man said. "I'm Inspector George Silver. I'm in charge of the investigation of Fred Leonardi's murder."

Angelo took a deep breath. "So you've come to arrest me."

Silver stared at him, but Angelo detected a humorous spark in his eyes. "Why would I want to arrest you?"

Angelo looked at him puzzled. "Well, I'm the prime suspect, am I not?"

Now Silver gave a quick smile. "You're right. You were the prime suspect ... until about a week ago."

"What happened?" Nicholas asked.

"There have been new developments. We have a confession from the killer."

Angelo, Sofia, and Nicholas looked at each other, then at the investigator.

"Who was it?" Angelo asked. "Anton Leonardi?"

"No, but he ordered the killing."

"I knew it," Angelo said, anger rising in him. "The bastard. He shot a man, and Fred and I witnessed it. That's why he killed him." The anger disappeared, replaced by relief. He was no longer a murder suspect.

Silver glared at Angelo. "Why didn't you report the murder? Why did you just disappear?"

Angelo lifted his arms, then lowered them again. "Many reasons. For one, I was terrified. I wasn't exactly a model citizen. Nobody would've believed me."

"We need you to make a statement," Silver said. "And because you're so good at disappearing, I want you to hand over your passport. You kind of remind me of Houdini, you know ... the old magician."

"I have no intention to disappear again." Angelo handed him the passport. "I hope I'll get it back. I do need to return to Italy, eventually."

"You'll get it back when you come to my office to make your statement," Silver said.

"What about Anton Leonardi?" Angelo asked.

"He's no longer a threat. This is the second piece of news," Silver said. "Anton Leonardi is dead."

"Dead?" Angelo looked at him stunned. "Somebody killed him?"

"No. He shot himself," Silver said.

There was a moment of shocked silence. "How? Why?" Sofia asked.

"I guess destiny finally caught up with him. He discovered he had terminal cancer and wouldn't live long."

Angelo's heart skipped a beat. The thought that the man from whom he had been hiding for so long was dead was only slowly registering in his mind. "My God. Well, I'd have to lie if I said I was sorry."

"I think nobody is sorry, except maybe his wife," Silver said. "We also have a statement from one of his mobster friends that he killed a man twenty years ago in California. It must be the murder you witnessed. In order to fully close the case, your statement is going to be very important."

Angelo took a deep breath. "I'm sorry I should've done it a long time ago."

"Perhaps you could've prevented further crimes, had you come forward." Silver touched him lightly on the shoulder. "But be this as it may. You're a free man."

Angelo cleared his throat. "I was involved in what I think was illegal work. We were transporting goods for Anton. I don't know for sure what it was, but it couldn't have been legal."

"Tell me about it in my office," Silver said. "The statute of limitation for smuggling contraband has probably expired after twenty years. Anyway, I'll let you go. There are some people from your family waiting for you."

Angelo glanced toward the exit. The emotions overwhelmed him when he recognized his brother.

Chapter 43

Martin and Maria had aged, of course. Martin was still tall and slim, now with gray-and-white hair instead of the dark hair Angelo remembered. Maria had gained some weight, but was as lovely as ever. Angelo's eyes teared up and he blinked as Martin walked toward him.

"Angelo," Martin said, his voice breaking.

The two brothers embraced for a long time. When they let go of each other, tears were coursing down their cheeks. They both pulled out handkerchiefs and wiped their faces, then gave embarrassed grins, and hugged again.

Angelo then turned to Maria and they hugged as well. "I'm so glad you're back," Maria said, her voice trembling slightly. Angelo inhaled her light lavender scent and it triggered a memory from a long time ago. Maria and Elvira had used the same body lotion. He sighed deeply at the memory of his wife. Her death had been another reason why he'd had to leave his ruined life behind.

Angelo looked at a young man and woman standing next to Maria, trying to remember who they were. He was short and sturdy with the same black eyes he himself had. Was it Nicholas's younger brother? "Matthew?" he asked.

The young man smiled. "Hello, Uncle Angelo. Yes, it's me. And you remember Nadia?" He put his arm around the young woman next to him. She was a little taller than Matthew, with wavy brown hair and green eyes.

"My God," Angelo said, trying to match the young woman with the little girl he barely remembered, the younger sister. "You were … like … how old are you now?"

"Twenty-two," Nadia said. She hugged him. "I have to admit I don't remember you."

"Of course not. You were only two when I left." Angelo shook his head. "It's only now I fully realize how long I've been away."

"Too long, *piccolo*," Martin said, using a term he used to call his brother as a child.

"Well, let's all go home and celebrate. I'm so glad they found the real culprits and you don't have to be afraid anymore." Maria took Angelo by the arm and they all walked to the cars.

"We had to come in two cars, since everybody wanted to be here," Martin said. "Well, almost everybody. Robert is away for a week on some wine publicity stunt, so he couldn't make it. Janice accompanied him."

"I heard he's quite the entrepreneur," Angelo said.

"Tell me about it," Martin said. "I don't know how he does it, but he's good at it."

At home, everybody gathered in Martin and Maria's house for a light dinner and to get acquainted again with Angelo.

He tried to come to terms with his thoughts and feelings. His mind was a beehive. Relief about the outcome of the investigation into Fred's murder, the death of Anton, the man who was one of the major reasons Angelo disappeared, took turns with feelings of confusion. He felt he was having an identity crisis. Here he was in a country and at a place he hadn't seen in twenty years, an environment that had changed tremendously. He'd had a glimpse of the proliferation of vineyards during the drive from the airport.

Twenty years before, there had only been a few from what he remembered. This was his home, or was it? Italy had become his home over the past twenty years, but only to a certain extent.

In Italy, he was Danilo Pedrotti, an impostor. His fake identity was only known to Abbot Francesco and now to Miriam. How would the people react if he finally told them his real name? Would he feel at home as Angelo Segantino in Rivalta? He believed his friends would understand once they heard why he had assumed a false identity. He had talked to Larry again who had told him that Fabio and his buddy in crime had been arrested, that no charges had been filed against the person who had shot Fabio in the leg. And best of all, Larry had gotten his old job back. Angelo smiled at the thought about the happy conversation he'd had with his friend.

"More ice cream, Angelo?" someone asked. It was Maria and she gave him an amused smile. "You're somewhere else with your thoughts, aren't you?"

Angelo took a deep breath. "Sorry, Maria, yes, I was thinking about … well, everything I guess. No more ice cream for me, thank you. Dinner was excellent."

"You're going to stay with us if that's okay," Martin said. "We have a nice guest room with a private bathroom."

"Thank you. This is a lot fancier than what I'm used to. My home in Italy is a cabin, more or less."

"But it's very beautiful," Sofia said. "A cozy cottage next to a lovely stone pine forest, a pond nearby, and it has a great view of the valley and the mountains."

Angelo nodded. "Miriam is taking care of it, while I'm gone," he said.

It was quiet for a few moments.

"You have to tell us a lot more about this mysterious Miriam," Nicholas said. "From what I heard, she was Sofia's partner in crime." He winked at Sofia.

"We became good friends," Sofia said. "I hope to see her again soon."

"Well, Angelo, you have to tell us all about it," Maria said. "But I can see you're fading. It's okay if you want to go to bed. I'll check to make sure there are towels and everything is ready."

"Thanks, Maria, yes, I'm getting sleepy. It's been a long day. I didn't get much sleep on the plane. I was too nervous. And, I can tell you, spending the night in this beautiful home is a lot better than in a jail cell."

"Thank, God, it didn't come to that," Martin said. He got up and patted Angelo on the back. "Glad you're back, little brother."

.

Chapter 44

The next few days, Angelo tried to familiarize himself with the home he had left, an environment that had changed so much. As he walked across the fields and looked at the vineyards of the Segantino family, memories cropped up of events and people from a long time ago. Sometimes he went alone on walks of discovery, often Martin and once in a while Nicholas and Sofia accompanied him.

Martin and Maria's home became a meeting place for the Segantino family. Robert and Janice, Nicholas's parents, returned from their trip. Robert was all enthusiastic about Angelo's return and implored him to stay. He offered him a job as administrator of his estate. Angelo was grateful for his nephew's attempt to help and promised to think about it. Truth was that he was confused and thrown off kilter by all the changes in the past few weeks.

"I have to get my bearings first," he kept saying. "I feel I've returned from another planet, in a way." Fortunately, they all understood and let him get used to everything.

One of the first things Angelo did was visit Elvira's grave in the town cemetery. He was surprised how well kept it was. Two potted plants and a vase with fresh spring flowers brightened the plot. The tombstone was clean and polished. Maria had told him that she had kept an eye on it during his absence. Angelo was moved by how well cared for and tidy it was.

He put a bouquet of flowers down—carnations, chrysanthemums, and yellow freesia, Elvira's favorites. He brushed his hand gently over the etching on the stone. Elvira Cynthia Segantino, March 3, 1950 to July 20, 1992.

"I'm sorry, Elvira," he whispered. "So sorry." A sob escaped him. To his relief, he was alone in the cemetery and could let his emotions take their course.

A few moments later, Angelo walked around the cemetery, looking for Fred's grave. As Martin had told him, Frank had been allowed to bury what was left of his brother after the investigation was over. Angelo found a newly planted plot with Fred's name on it. He stood in front of the grave for a while, then put down a small potted plant.

"Hey, buddy, I know you probably would've preferred a cold beer." Angelo exhaled deeply. "I'm so sorry, Fred. You should be here with me. I hope that wherever you are, you're at peace. But it's just not right."

He heard the sound of heavy footsteps behind him and turned around. He barely recognized the overweight man with the curly gray hair and the red face. "Frank?"

Frank nodded. "Hi, Angelo."

There was an awkward moment. Frank cleared his throat. "I apologize for thinking you killed Fred."

Angelo shook his head. "You don't have to apologize. If I'd been you, I would've thought the same. I wasn't exactly a model citizen."

"No, that's right, but neither was Fred," Frank said. "And least of all, Anton."

They stood silently for a while, looking at Fred's grave.

"You know, one of the things I don't understand," Angelo said. "How was it possible for Anton or his hired hand to bury Fred's body on your property without anybody hearing or seeing anything?"

Frank shrugged. "I've asked myself the same, but I can see now how it happened." He motioned with his head to a bench at the edge of the cemetery. "Let's sit down for a while."

They walked over and sat on a stone bench under one of the oak trees. Frank removed his baseball cap and wiped his forehead. He exuded a light smell of sweat. *He looks like a candidate for a heart attack.*

"At the time when you and Fred disappeared, it was only myself and our uncle, Sam Leonardi, working the farm. Fred was off doing his own thing and Anton wasn't around much anymore." Frank put his hat back on.

"Uncle Sam was hard of hearing and my bedroom was to the back of the house. So, really, anybody who knew the property could've come at night and buried the body. The field he was buried in was at the edge of our farm, well, next to your family's land. It wasn't used. It was overgrown and nobody came by much."

Angelo nodded. It made sense.

"I remember Fred coming home from one of his jobs, delivering stuff for Anton," Frank continued. "He was all upset. He didn't say what happened, but he got into a huge argument with our uncle. Fred said he was leaving, he'd had enough of Sam bullying him.

"I have to admit," Frank went on. "Sam Leonardi was a tough and sometimes cruel father and uncle. He took the belt to us many times when we were kids. But he was fair. And he provided for Fred and me. As you probably remember, our parents died when we were still little and Sam took us in and treated us like his sons." Frank pulled out a pack of cigarettes from his pocket and offered Angelo one. Angelo declined.

"Anyway, the following day, Fred was gone. He had taken a bag with some clothes, but not much. We assumed he was just pissed off and went to stay with one of his friends, you or even Anton. He'd done it before when he got into a fight with our uncle." Frank lit his cigarette. He squeezed his eyes shut and blew the smoke through his nose.

"We weren't too concerned, but when Fred didn't come back and we didn't hear from him, Sam went over to talk to your brother. Martin told us that you had disappeared as well and they had no idea where you were. I think both families were pretty much convinced that you were both involved in some criminal activities and kind of washed their hands of you."

Angelo gave a grunt. "I don't blame them."

"Well, yes. On top of it, Anton wasn't around anywhere either. The next we heard from him was that he'd moved to Chicago. We thought that perhaps you and Fred were there as well."

Angelo shook his head. "You never tried to find him after that?"

"We did, at least I did. Sam said he didn't care, he didn't want anything to do with his loser son and nephew anymore. I went to Chicago, tried to track down Anton but didn't find him. I went to the police, filed a missing person's report. But nothing came of it. So, I finally gave up. I have to admit, I didn't get along with Fred much. See, I was resentful. I did all the work at the farm, when our uncle got older. I had to watch how Fred did nothing to help me, but came home with money from what I thought were his illegal dealings. Just like you."

Angelo lowered his head. "Yes, I'm not proud of that part of my life, believe me."

"Well, at least you turned your life around. Fred didn't have a chance to do it." Frank sounded bitter.

"I'm sorry, Frank, I wish it had turned out differently." Angelo gazed at the oak trees in the field next to the cemetery. "I still don't understand why Anton had the body buried on the family property. Wasn't he afraid, someone was going to use the field, dig it up to plant something?"

Frank sneered. "Well, for one thing, Anton expected to inherit the family property after his father's death. He figured his dirty secret was safe. See, that piece of property isn't worth much for the kind of farming we did. It was too rocky, too much gravel and flint. But of course, it's perfect for grapes and wine. That's why your great-nephew and his wife bought it."

"Makes sense," Angelo said. "But once he knew that you inherited it, wasn't he afraid you might dig it up or sell it?"

"Sure, after he found out that I inherited the land, he was furious," Frank said. "I felt kind of bad for him. I told him I wouldn't mind sharing if he decided to move back and help me work the property. I knew he wouldn't go for it. He told me he had no time or interest in farming. The only thing he asked me was that if I ever wanted to sell it or part of it, to let him know. He wanted to have first buying rights."

Frank removed his cap and scratched his head. "I kind of wondered why he would want to buy land from a farm he had no interest in. I thought it was just for the money, that he would sell it again. Now, I know why he wanted to prevent me from selling the field Fred was buried in."

"But you did sell the field to Nicholas and Sofia. I assume Anton didn't know about it?"

"No, not right away. Only after Fred's bones were found. I hadn't heard from Anton in … oh … over ten years. I didn't even think he'd be interested anymore. I actually tried to call him before I finalized the sale, but couldn't get a hold of him. So I told myself, to heck with it. After my wife died and the boys moved away, the farm was getting too big for me anyway. So I sold the field. It's perfect for grapes, but not for much else."

"Sofia and Nicholas certainly appreciate it. They're eager to plant, now that everything has been settled. I'm sure they'll let you have some of their wine," Angelo said.

"Well, I'm not much into wine. I prefer a good bottle of beer," Frank said.

"Just like Fred, as I remember," Angelo said.

"Yeah." Frank sighed.

Angelo put his hand on Frank's back. "Frank, I'm sorry about what happened to Fred. We did some dumb things together. But he was a good friend, and I miss him."

"Thanks." Frank nodded.

"I'm glad you and the Segantinos are talking to each other again. I know Martin really regretted the bad blood between the families," Angelo said.

"Yeah. I'm glad, too," Frank said. "I mean, neighbors have to get along."

It was quiet again. Angelo patted Frank's shoulder, then got up. Frank groaned a little as he raised himself and wiped his forehead again. "What are you going to do? Stay here or go back to Italy?"

Angelo shrugged. "I need to go back. I have a lot of unresolved business there. Right now, I don't know where I'm going to live in the future. Time will tell."

"Well, good to see you again." Frank waved goodbye and left.

Angelo watched him slowly making his way through the cemetery. He felt sorry for Frank. He seemed lonely.

.

Chapter 45

"I ran into Frank Leonardi," Angelo said, when he came back from his visit to the cemetery.

"Oh, yes?" Martin raised an eyebrow. "How did that go?"

"Fine. He apologized for having suspected me of killing Fred."

"Oh, I guess he truly had a change of heart. He came by here to apologize to us as well," Martin said.

"He seems lonely." Angelo told Martin and Maria about their talk.

"Yes, he's had a hard time since his wife died. Also, he's not in good health, and the farm is getting to be too much for him," Maria said. "At least, his sons come by frequently and they seem to be close."

She went into the kitchen and came back with glasses and a bottle of wine. "I'm glad we reestablished some kind of pleasant relationship again. We felt really bad, not being on speaking terms with him."

"True," Martin said. "It must be hard for Frank to lose his cousin and his brother like this, one of them a killer who commits suicide and the other one being murdered by the first."

The door opened and Nicholas and Sofia came in. "We just saw Frank Leonardi. He was very friendly and asked us how we're doing with our new field," Nicholas said.

Angelo told them about running into him at the cemetery and Martin mentioned that Frank had apologized to him and Maria as well.

"I still wonder if he was the one who organized the break-in at our house." Nicholas narrowed his eyes. "Did he say anything?"

Maria shook her head. "No, he didn't and we may never know. I still think it was him, or rather someone he hired to search for the diary. What else could it have been?"

"Yes, well nothing has happened since, so I hope that was it," Nicholas said.

"What break-in?" Angelo asked.

"That's right, we haven't told you yet." Nicholas glanced at Martin.

"I wanted to wait until Silver gave us back Elvira's diary," Martin said.

Angelo felt a jolt in his stomach. "Elvira's diary?"

"Yes," Martin gave him a worried look. "I hope this isn't too much of a shock. Sofia found a diary when she cleaned out the storage room in their place, you know the house you and Elvira lived in for a while. The diary belonged to Elvira. We read it, hoping to find some clues about what happened that made you disappear so suddenly."

"Oh, God," Angelo said. He sat down and covered his face with his hands, then looked up again. "Was it … painful to read? I caused her so much grief."

"Well …" Martin hesitated. "She worried about you, about the stuff you got involved in."

Angelo exhaled deeply. "I don't know if I want to read it."

"We're sorry we read it, Angelo," Maria said. "It seemed the only way to get some possible clues of your whereabouts."

"I don't mind that you read it," Angelo said. "You all know about my screwed-up life back then. But of all the things I regret the most is the way I treated Elvira." Angelo's voice trembled.

Sofia put her hand on Angelo's shoulder. "She was just very worried about you. But we also found something positive. There was a bundle of letters, love letters you wrote to her that she kept. I only read one," Sofia hurried to say.

"I remember, I did write her a few letters." Angelo gave a quick chortle. "It feels as if my past, the past that I ran from, is attacking me full force."

"You can't run away from the past. But you came back to face it. Now it's time to move on," Martin said.

"You're right, but it will take me a while," Angelo said.

They all sat down to a dinner of barbecued steak, baked potato, and salad. "We need to get Angelo used to an all-American meal again. Forget pasta and risotto for a while," Martin said with a twinkle in his eyes as he brought in the steaks from the grill on the patio.

Maria distributed the baked potatoes and sour cream, and passed around the salad bowl.

"Nothing wrong with a juicy steak," Angelo said. He inhaled the scent of grilled meat and a smile spread across his face. It was good to be back.

After dinner, they sat on the patio. It had been a hot day, and the warmth lingered into the evening. It smelled of sagebrush mixed with whiffs from the fire in the barbecue. Angelo took a deep breath and glanced at Sofia.

"I forgot to tell you Miriam says hello."

"Ah, the mysterious Miriam. You have to tell us about her," Maria said. "Wait, until I get the cake. It's easier to talk over dessert."

Sofia and Maria brought back a homemade chocolate cake and a pot of coffee. While they ate, Angelo told them about Miriam, how he met her and that he left her behind because he was afraid his presence might endanger her life.

"And now?" Maria asked, after Angelo finished his story.

"I hope she has forgiven me for abandoning her," Angelo said.

"Well, and?" Maria sounded impatient. "Is there the possibility of a romance?"

"I know Miriam still loves him," Sofia said.

Angelo shook his head and grinned. "You're a bunch of hopeless romantics. I'm sixty-five years old. I have nothing to offer a woman. I don't even know what I'm going to live on when I get even older. I have some savings, but that won't get me very far. I can't expect a woman to share her life with me."

"Oh, fiddlesticks. If you love each other, you'll find ways," Maria said.

"Well, Angelo, you will have options if you decide to live here," Martin said. "We are family and we support each other."

"No, Martin, you've supported me enough and look how I paid you back." Angelo said gruffly.

"That's in the past. You've become a different person. It's obvious." Martin coughed. "And I say this also for selfish reasons. I'd like to have you around in my old age. We missed so much of each other's lives. And it wasn't only your fault. I didn't try very hard to find you when you disappeared. I was angry and resentful and judged you too harshly."

"No, you didn't. I deserved your contempt. I've disappointed you many times over the years when you tried to help me get out of the mess I put myself in," Angelo protested.

"All right, you two. You have admitted and regretted your faults and now it's time to put it all behind you. End of confessions," Maria said with a stern voice, then tittered.

"Yes, Ma'am," Angelo and Martin said in unison.

Chapter 46

Martin accompanied Angelo to George Silver's office. Angelo made and signed a statement so the police could officially close the case against Anton Leonardi. It was mainly a formality, but for Angelo, it meant an end to a life of hiding and running. A burden lifted off his shoulders and his heart felt lighter.

No mention was made of Angelo and Fred's illegal work twenty years before. Silver returned his passport and wished him a good trip back. There was a tense moment when the investigator handed Angelo Elvira's diary. Angelo's hand trembled when he took it.

"Are you going to read it?" Martin asked him as they were driving home.

"I don't know." Angelo glanced at the notebook he held tenderly in his hands, as if it was part of his wife. "A diary is something private, isn't it? It's really just for the person who writes it." He paused. "Or is this just an excuse because I'm afraid to read it?"

"You don't need to read it. Those are Elvira's personal thoughts. I felt guilty reading it, but we had no choice. But just to put your mind at rest. Elvira was worried about you, but she didn't hate you. She loved you. And if reading it would just awaken your regret and guilt again, let it be. She is at peace and you've started a new life. Why dig in old stuff?"

Angelo nodded. "You're right."

Two weeks later, the family took Angelo to the airport for his flight back to Italy. Martin wished to have his younger brother around for a longer time. Angelo promised to keep in touch and to come back at least for a visit soon. And Maria and Martin were planning a trip to Italy as well. The sadness of seeing Angelo leave was somewhat tempered by the knowledge that he was alive and well.

Now, they were at the airport and Martin tried to think positive thoughts. He'd see his brother again one way or the other. They would keep in touch by phone or email. Of course, he hoped that Angelo would decide to move back to the United States. He had even checked with Medicare and Social Security and found out that Angelo had just enough credits from the years he worked here to qualify for some social security benefits and, what was even more important, he was eligible to join Medicare.

"I'll think about it," Angelo had said. Martin knew that he had to accept his brother's decision. But when they hugged goodbye and he saw him walk through customs waving at them, Martin felt a knot in his throat.

"Are you okay, honey?" Maria put her arm around him. "He'll be back."

Martin nodded. "I know." He blinked the rising tears away. "And if not, we're going to track him down. After all, we have a private investigator in the family now."

Sofia chuckled. "Don't you worry. Miriam and I will find him again. Promise."

"Excuse me?" Nicholas glared at her and raised an eyebrow.

"Oh, sorry." Sofia grinned. "*Nicholas*, Miriam and I, of course."

"That's better," Nicholas grumbled.

Back home, Sofia and Nicholas focused again on the work at the vineyard. They had taken time out to be with their great-uncle and now had to get back to racking the aging wine from former harvests and checking the vines and ripening grapes in preparation for the next one. Martin worked together with them, although Nicholas said, it wasn't necessary.

"Helps me keep my mind on the vineyards and not feel homesick for my brother," he said.

"Wasn't it wonderful how it turned out though?" Nicholas touched Martin's arm. "He's alive and well and you are in touch again."

"Yes, of course," Martin said. "I still can't believe it. I almost got used to the thought that I'd never see him again. Even now, there are moments when I worry that somehow the same thing or something similar will happen again."

"How do you mean?" Sofia asked. She lifted one of the grape vine leaves to check on a cluster of grapes.

"I've been so used to my younger brother being involved in illegal and questionable activities that there is still this slight feeling of distrust. I know it's unfair and it's my problem not his."

"I think he's on the right path now though," Sofia said. "During the time I spent with him, I experienced him as a truly good person. And even Miriam who had known him for a few years didn't say anything to the contrary. She was upset with him for leaving her, but we know now why he did it."

Martin nodded. "You're right. You met the changed Angelo, whereas I still carry the baggage of his past. I need to let go of it."

Chapter 47

"Thanksgiving." Sofia smiled, as she opened the window, inhaling the nippy late fall air. The fog still hovered over the fields, but a few sun rays penetrated the fading mist. It was a cool but sunny day. She sniffed. No, it wasn't the smell of the turkey sizzling in the oven yet. It was the scent of moist grass and soil soaked by the mist and dew, an earthy fall smell.

Thanksgiving was her favorite holiday. She even liked it better than Christmas. It was a family get-together without the pressure of trying to decide what gifts to give to people who already had everything. It was also a time to give thanks. And in the Segantino family, there was plenty to be thankful for this year: the reunion of Angelo with his family, and, of course, having her sister Julietta with her, and important other news.

Sofia and Nicholas had picked Julietta up at the airport two weeks before. Julietta would spend the holidays with them and then start her studies at Cal Poly in the spring.

The Thanksgiving meal took place at the grandparents. Martin and Maria and Nicholas's parents usually took turns inviting people for the feast. This year, however, Robert, Janice, and Nicholas's brother and sister spent Thanksgiving with Janice's family. To Sofia's disappointment, Emma, her aunt who lived in Santa Monica and had spent last Thanksgiving with them, was celebrating with Sofia's grandparents in Vermont. But she would be back for Christmas.

In the kitchen, Sofia poured herself a cup of coffee. Nicholas had already left to do some last-minute grocery shopping with Martin. Sofia and Julietta were going to help Maria prepare dinner.

"Ah, coffee," Julietta said, as she came out of her room. She picked up a cup and put it under the spout of the espresso machine.

Sofia and Julietta had been to Cal Poly a few times to get Julietta ready for her classes in the spring. She had met with the counselor who had helped her select her courses. During an informal meeting with other students, she had met a few young men and women, also from Europe. Now, she felt more relaxed and was looking forward to her studies.

"Thank God, help is here," Maria said when Sofia and Julietta entered the kitchen. She pulled a handkerchief out of her apron pocket and wiped her sweaty face. "I think I'm getting too old for preparing such a feast."

"That's why we're here," Sofia said. She and Julietta took over at the stove, stirring the green beans and the gravy, and mashing the potatoes.

Martin and Maria pulled the heavy turkey out of the oven. Nicholas volunteered to slice the bird. Maria, Julietta, and Sofia carried the green beans, yams, mashed potatoes, and cranberries into the living room. Delicious smells permeated the home.

When everything was ready, they all sat around the table in the dining area. Martin and Nicholas poured glasses of Sangiovese from their estate. After saying thanks, Martin lifted his glass and everybody wished each other a happy Thanksgiving. Sofia took a little sip of her wine, then put the glass down and smiled at Nicholas.

Everybody was in good spirits. Sofia noticed that Martin was in a particularly animated mood. The normally quiet and somewhat serious man was outright chatty. He told Julietta a few funny stories about his time at the university.

They also discussed plans for the following year. Now that the problems with the new field were resolved, Nicholas and Sofia looked forward to planting their Zinfandel vines in spring.

After a plentiful and satisfying meal, they sat in the living room next to a roaring fire in the fireplace, enjoying the traditional pumpkin pie with whipped cream and sipping coffee. Martin got up and reached for a large envelope on the buffet.

"I have news for you," he said, a smile spreading across his face. He pulled some papers out of the envelope and a couple of photos.

"What is it?" Nicholas asked.

"You'll see," Maria smiled as well.

Martin handed Sofia and Nicholas the photos. Sofia glanced at one of the picture, then exclaimed, "Miriam and Angelo … all dressed up. This looks like a special occasion … is this what I think it is?" She handed the photo to Nicholas.

Maria laughed. "Yes, they got married."

"Oh, how wonderful," Sofia said. "I was really hoping they'd get together again, but getting married. That's even better."

"Look at them." Nicholas showed Sofia the other picture. "She must be quite a bit younger than he is."

"Yes, that's true," Sofia said.

"He's robbing the cradle, the devil." Nicholas laughed.

"Well, there's more," Martin said and handed Nicholas a piece of paper. It was a letter. Sofia and Nicholas read it together.

Dear Maria and Martin, dear family,

As you can see from the photos, Miriam and I embarked on a special adventure. We tied the knot. When I got back, I went to her and asked her to marry me. I don't know what drove me to be so bold, considering I'd treated her quite badly in the past. And I still can't believe she actually agreed! But she did. That's the first piece of good news.

The second one: we are planning to move back to the United States next year, most likely in spring sometime. I received an offer (well, more like an order) from Abbot Francesco of the Novalesa Abbey to work together with its sister abbey in San Luis Obispo. I'm going to be in charge of a similar program for young people as we have here. And Miriam has the possibility to work at a day care center in the same town.

We're looking forward to the move, although it won't be easy to say goodbye to Italy and our friends. But we'll be in touch with the abbey here, and I'll be traveling back and forth at least for a while.

I hope this is good news and won't shock you too much. We'll talk on the phone in a couple of days and I'll explain everything.

In the meantime, we're wishing you and the whole family a Happy Thanksgiving and a joyful Holiday Season. Next year, we'll be able to celebrate together.

Thinking of you with love and gratitude,
Angelo and Miriam

"Wow, no wonder you're in such a good mood, Grandpa," Nicholas said.

"Yes, we're very happy about it." Martin's face gleamed with joy.

It was quiet for a while, with everybody digesting the news. Then, Nicholas took a sip of espresso and cleared his throat.

"Well, now, what about a third piece of good news?" He put his arm around Sofia. "Do you want to tell them?"

Sofia nodded. "Yes. You may have wondered why I'm not drinking much wine tonight." Sofia raised her glass of lemonade. "Well, in seven months, if everything goes well, there will be a new family member. I'm two months pregnant."

There was an explosion of jubilation and laughter. Maria and Martin hugged Sofia and Nicholas.

"This will be my first niece or nephew," Julietta said, beaming with joy.

"Wait," Martin scrunched his forehead. "Does this mean, what I think it means? I'm going to be a great-grandfather? This sounds quite old. Oh, my."

Maria laughed. "You'll get used to it, Grandpa."

Later that night, after clearing away the dishes and helping Maria clean up, they sat in the living room, enjoying the last of the fire in the fireplace.

"This is a true Thanksgiving," Maria said. "So much to be thankful for."

"A lot of wonderful things have happened this year, that's for sure." Martin put his arm around Maria. "Finding Angelo is one of them. Sometimes, I still can't believe it."

"I know what you mean," Maria said. "But I think even more important is that Angelo found himself. His true self. He's come a long long way."

The End

Acknowledgements

Heartfelt thanks to the many people who have in one way or the other contributed to this book. It would be impossible to list them all. But here are a few I am especially grateful to. I truly appreciate my precious beta readers and their helpful suggestions. Thank you Silvia Delorenzi for correcting my faulty Italian and for the careful observations. Thank you to my family in Switzerland, who accompanied me on my travels to the beautiful Piedmont in Italy. I am deeply grateful to Linda Cassidy Lewis, my editor, for her keen eye and excellent feedback and to Lisette Brodey, who spotted those blunders we all missed. And last, but not least, thank you, Diane Busch, for another lovely cover.

Christa Polkinhorn, originally from Switzerland, lives and works as writer and translator in the Los Angeles area in California. She divides her time between the United States and Switzerland and has strong ties to both countries. She is the author of six novels and a collection of poems. Her travels and her interest in foreign cultures inform her work and her novels take place in several countries. Aside from writing and traveling, she is an avid reader and a lover of the arts, dark chocolate, and red wine.